I LOVE A LASS

Elizabeth Cadell

D1546380

Chivers Press • Thorndike Press
Bath, Avon, England   Thorndike, Maine USA

This Large Print edition is published by Chivers Press, England, and by Thorndike Press, USA.

Published in 1994 in the U.K. by arrangement with the author's estate.

Published in 1994 in the U.S. by arrangement with Brandt & Brandt Literary Agents, Inc.

U.K. Hardcover ISBN 0–7451–2397–X (Chivers Large Print)
U.K. Softcover   ISBN 0–7451–2399–6 (Camden Large Print)
U.S. Softcover   ISBN 0–7862–0286–6 (General Series Edition)

The text of this Large Print edition is unabridged.
Other aspects of the book may vary from the original edition.

Set in 16pt. News Plantin.

Printed in the U.K. on acid-free paper.

British Library Cataloguing in Publication Data available

Library of Congress Cataloging-in-Publication Data

Cadell, Elizabeth.
  I love a lass / Elizabeth Cadell.
    p. cm.
  ISBN 0–7862–0286–6 (alk. paper : lg print)
  1. Large type books.   I. Title.
[PR6005.A225I2   1994]
823′.914—dc20
                                           94–20457

CHAPTER ONE

The crossing had been far from pleasant. The steamer began its journey in the shelter of Southampton Water, but the calm deceived none of the passengers; the weather reports had made everybody only too certain of what awaited them in the English Channel. State of sea: rough, the *Times* had stated uncompromisingly, and rough it was. The September night came down and veiled the miseries of those on deck; in the cabins below, sleepless travellers lay counting the uncomfortable hours that must elapse before the ship reached St Malo and delivered them upon the fair—and firm—land of France.

Few on board remained indifferent or oblivious to the violent movements of the little vessel, but Sebastian Page, in one of the more luxurious single berth cabins, slept soundly throughout the night. He had driven down from London, embarked himself and his car, eaten a good dinner, undressed and gone to bed. The rolling and pitching of the ship, if he felt it at all, served only to lull him to deeper slumber.

In the morning, a steward roused him with tea. Sebastian yawned, stretched, sat up and put a lazy question.

'How long before we're in?'

1

'Matter of half an hour, sir. The ship's steadied up a lot.'

'Rough night, was it?'

'It ... well, yes; she danced about a bit, sir. You didn't feel it?'

'Didn't feel a thing.'

The steward retired, not unimpressed; he had been attending the afflicted throughout the night, and Number 62, untroubled in expensive grey silk pyjamas, clear-eyed after a sound night's rest, presented a picture very different from the painful ones he had been witnessing. He closed the door with respect and Sebastian drank the tea, dressed and went up on deck. There he found sunshine and a tossing, blue-and-white sea and received the pleasant impression that St Malo, acting on behalf of all France, was rushing forward eagerly to welcome him.

He leaned against the rail and let his eyes roam over the familiar beaches of Dinard. He was a tall man of about thirty-four, dark, good-looking, with a slight air of aloofness; surrounded by fellow-passengers, he gave no sign of being aware that there was anybody on the deck but himself. His eyes, glancing round casually, held only the reflection of his own thoughts; when he walked away from the rail, he edged round human obstructions without appearing to see them, and the fact that he did so with quiet courtesy did nothing to allay the vague feelings of resentment he left behind

2

him.

Sebastian's thoughts were not, in fact, on his present surroundings; he was contemplating the immediate future, which held some pleasant prospects. He glanced briefly at the seamen engaged in opening the hold; down there, he mused happily, was Betsy, waiting for a chance to show what she could do on the fast roads of Europe. France, Germany, Scandinavia; no hard-and-fast programme, he and Joss had decided. Their plan was simply to drive Betsy as far and as speedily as possible in the two weeks at their disposal—or, more accurately, at Joss's disposal; Sebastian's time was his own. This was not to be a sightseeing tour; he and Joss had seen a good deal of Europe and would see a good deal more—some other time. On this trip, the sight to interest them most would be the three-figure indications on Betsy's speedometer.

He glanced over his shoulder at the steamer's turbulent wake and then beyond it to the white-flecked sea over which the boat from the island of Jersey was approaching St Malo. It was due to arrive at half-past ten; by noon, Sebastian calculated, he and Joss would be on their way.

Joss ... A smile hovered on his lips. Good old Joss. It would be good to see him again.

They were good friends, but they met only two or three times a year. That they had met at all was due to the accident of war, which had brought them together for three years in close and well-tried companionship, bridging a gap unlikely to have been crossed in the ordinary course of their lives. Sebastian was the only son of wealthy and titled parents and moved along paths on which the primrose would have looked out of place. Joss was by profession an accountant, the son of nobody in particular, a man of simple and inexpensive habits. Financially, they were poles apart; physically, only the English Channel separated them. Sebastian lived for the most part in London, while Joss owned a little cottage of Jersey granite perched on a slope overlooking the Corbière lighthouse.

Joss had been surprised at the durability of the friendship. Without illusions, he had given it, in his own mind, a time limit. The limit had been reached and passed and Sebastian still sought him out, still claimed most of his vacations; they still enjoyed one another's company on trips abroad in Sebastian's sports cars, of which Betsy was the latest and fastest. Sebastian still descended upon the cottage for unheralded visits; Joss received him calmly, left him to amuse himself and went on leading his own uneventful existence. Each thought the other's way of life dull in the extreme, but their admiration for one another, unvoiced, persisted. Sebastian envied Joss's easy, casual acceptance of things as they came; Joss found peculiar pride in the knowledge that Sebastian, with all the odds against him, remained essentially unspoiled.

The ship bumped gently once and then again, and Sebastian came out of his reverie to find that it was parked, to all appearances, on a street in St Malo. A few feet away stood French policemen, French porters and a miscellany of French citizens. Family groups clustered beyond the barrier, waving and shouting to their relatives on board; the gangway was being placed in position. Sebastian felt a surge of keen anticipation; he was here, Betsy was here, Joss would soon be here and they would soon be off.

And speaking of getting off, why, he wondered, did people have this unaccountable desire to be first off the ship? Why did they load themselves with hand luggage and push frantically in an effort to squeeze themselves through the throng? Why didn't that elderly woman in black, for example, sit down and rest until the gangway was in position and she could go comfortably ashore? Why dig her elbows into neighbouring ribs and tread on intervening toes when by merely waiting a few minutes she could disembark with dignity? What was the rush? The Paris train didn't leave for another couple of hours; the coaches lined up waiting for excursionists could wait a little longer; why stampede?

He stood leaning against the rail for some time, making no effort to disembark, watching the busy scene below and amusing himself by contrasting the noisy and gesticulating groups with the comparatively phlegmatic types he had observed at Southampton the night before. This, he considered, was all very French; some of those fellows down there seemed to be angry, some exasperated, but they were all plainly overexcited. Temperament. Nor did the temperament seem to be confined to the dock area; everywhere on the road people seemed to be gathering to discuss some important news.

His curiosity stirred, Sebastian at last went below, saw his luggage carried out and followed it down the gangway. The majority of the passengers were ashore; he threaded his way to the Customs shed, passing the tourists who were being rounded up for the Mont-St-Michel tour and those who were being shepherded to the coach for La Baule. He had his luggage placed on the counter near a Customs official, and then found that nobody was displaying any great eagerness to clear passengers' baggage; the Customs officials, like their compatriots, were in a group, arguing and gesticulating.

Sebastian addressed the porter who was waiting for his cleared luggage.

'What passes?' he enquired.

'It is a strike, monsieur. There are no trains; the trains have stopped; the trains will not go because those who drive them will not drive them. There are no trains. It is a strike.'

That, reflected Sebastian, made it reasonably clear. Well, it was bad luck for those who needed trains, but for himself it was no headache; Betsy would soon be hoisted aloft, set gently down again on French soil, and he and Joss would be in her and away.

He looked about him, estimating the number of passengers affected by the strike, and found that they constituted the large majority. Couriers were herding the last parties into coaches; the owners of private cars collected those they had come to meet and took them away. Those travelling by train remained, disorganized, distracted. Some were straining their inadequate French in an attempt to get a clearer idea of the situation, some were agitated, some frankly panic-stricken. Sebastian, walking about and gleaning items of information as he went, concluded that the strike was general and not local; there would be no trains that day, none perhaps for days to come. Excitement was mounting; the clamour increased; strike leaders, mounted on boxes or on benches, were addressing the workers.

Sebastian walked across to one of the groups to hear what was being said, but before he reached it, he found his path barred by the large, elderly, black-clad woman he had noticed pushing her way to the gangway. She planted herself squarely before him and addressed him in strongly accented English.

'You came on the boat?'

She spoke without a trace of apology in her tone. Her manner was imperious. Sebastian lifted his eyebrows at the lack of ceremony with which she had stopped him, and answered coldly.

'I did, madame.'

He moved a step backward as he spoke; she was too close. He had an impression, that he did not care to make more detailed, of shabbiness and slovenliness. He would have moved away, but something in her determined air told him that she would follow him and press her questions.

'You are going by train?'

'No, madame.'

'Then by what? You have a car?'

'I have.' And if you think you're going to set one foot in Betsy, he added to himself, you can think again.

'What car?' she demanded. 'A big car? Is it full?'

'Quite full, madame. It holds only two: my friend and myself.'

He was surprised at the chilliness of his tone. He was moved, as a rule, by a feeling that old ladies, young children and immature girls merited the same approach: a kindly manner concealing abysmal boredom. But there was something about this uninhibited stranger that roused an aversion he saw little reason to

8

conceal.

'You wonder why I ask? Well, I will tell you,' she said. 'I have business, urgent business. I must have a conveyance. I was taking the train, but now there is this strike. I am going to Lysaine—have you heard of Lysaine?'

'I'm afraid I haven't, madame. If you'll excuse me—'

'Please pay attention.' The calm authority in her tone made him stiffen angrily. 'I have to go to Lysaine, which is not more than two hundred kilometres from this place. If you will take me, I will pay you for your car. Which is more, I will—'

'I am extremely sorry, but—'

'I will pay you well. I wish to get there soon, today, this morning or this afternoon. I have business at my chateau.'

Sebastian eyed her. Delusions, was his first thought, and then something in her bearing, in her face, gave him pause. She had keen little black eyes, flabby, high-boned cheeks and a long, impressively arched nose. It was the nose that convinced Sebastian. It was a nose of authority; the eyes, set rather close together, seemed to peer down it haughtily. It was pointing up at him now like a spear held to his breast, pinning him down until this matter of transport was arranged.

With an effort, he summoned his resolution. He addressed her in French.

'There is no possibility, madame, of my

9

giving you a lift. I regret. When my car is put ashore, I—'

'You need not speak to me in French,' she told him angrily. 'My English is perfectly good enough. And shall I tell you something? You may be saying the truth, that there will be no possibility of taking me in your car. When you speak of having this car of yours, you speak with perhaps too much confidence. I asked you to take me to my chateau, but if you had agreed to do this, perhaps you would have found, after all, that you could not do it. You know why? Go and find out. Go there and listen to what those men are saying; your French is good, and so you will understand. They are Communists—you will see. And they are saying that the men who work here, here on the dock, should also make a strike. And if this happens, you will not get your car. No. The car will not be taken out of the ship. Look behind you; already they are refusing to work. You see? I think that you will not get your car. But I have another idea. Please pay attention. I have thought that—'

But Sebastian was no longer listening. With a slight bow, he had stepped round her and was walking rapidly and uneasily towards the ship. He went up the gangway and peered incredulously down at the cars, at the waiting Betsy, at the men hanging round the open hatch, at the unmanned cranes, at the workmen idle on shore. Disbelief became apprehension, apprehension certainty. The strike had spread. Work had ceased. The cars were not being unloaded; Betsy would not be lifted on to French soil; she would not streak up the great motor roads of Europe, flicking contemptuously past lesser vehicles. Betsy was down there—strike-bound.

When the boat from Jersey docked, Sebastian was standing on the quay scanning the decks for a sight of Joss; when he located him among the crowd on deck, he walked to a point from which he could speak to him. Joss leaned over the rail with a question.

'What's this about a strike?'

Sebastian hunched his shoulders in a gesture of helplessness. 'It's true. I don't think we're going to get Betsy off the ship.'

There was no comment from Joss; Sebastian had not expected one. Joss had a restful way of saying nothing when there was nothing to be said. Instead, he leaned against the rail and studied the scene below him—a long, lean, quiet man, brown-haired, grey-eyed, outwardly more serious than Sebastian, inwardly perhaps the more humorous of the two. When the first rush of disembarking passengers was over, he came down the gangway and joined Sebastian. With him, to Sebastian's surprise, came a fair-haired little boy of about six, who negotiated the gangway in a series of hops, keeping all the while a firm hold on Joss.

'Who've you got there?' enquired Sebastian, when the two had joined him.

'I've got to hand him over to his relations—aunt and grandfather, as far as I can make out.'

'Who is he?'

'No idea,' said Joss. 'His mother came up to me on the quay at St Helier just before the boat left and asked if I'd see that he got ashore and joined up with Tante somebody and Grandpère. I'll have to go and look for them.'

'What's his name?'

'Maurice something. Maurice,' directed Joss, 'skip off and see if you can see your grandfather or your aunt.'

'I'll bring them here to you,' promised Maurice, and darted away. The two men studied one another.

'Well, how was the trip?' asked Joss.

'They told me it was rough. I slept. What time did you leave Jersey?'

'Seven-thirty.'

'Seasick?'

'No. I stayed up on deck and walked about. It was only three hours.'

He paused; Sebastian did not appear to be listening; his eyes and his mind were on something else. Joss made an attempt to regain his attention.

'How serious is this strike?' he asked.

'Mm?'

'I said, how serious is this strike. Strike. A strike. A blow. A blow on the other fellow's

12

chin to teach him to listen when spoken to. Strike.'

'Oh, strike!' Sebastian's attention returned momentarily. 'I'll talk about that in a moment. Look, Joss, who's that girl over there?'

Joss, with a lift of his eyebrows, followed the direction of the other's glance.

'Oh, her? What makes you think I'd know?' he asked.

'She got off your boat, the Jersey boat. I watched her disembark. Very pretty it was, too. You must know who she is.'

'Why?'

'Because, dammit, Jersey is an island measuring about fifty or sixty square miles, isn't it?'

'Roughly.'

'And there's only one place on it that could rank as a town, isn't there?'

'St Helier. Correct.'

'All right then. A girl as lovely as that one couldn't appear in any town without causing a riot. Come on, come on; talk.'

'She moves,' said Joss, 'in ducal circles. Jersey, as I don't have to remind you, is full of dukes and barons and so on, with a few millionaires for makeweight. She circulates among them.'

'You can present me,' said Sebastian.

'I've just told you, I don't know the girl. She's out of my reach. I once met her father—briefly—and neither of us enjoyed the

13

experience. Now will you tell me what you know about this strike?'

'It's serious and we can't get Betsy unloaded. Who's that fellow she's talking to?'

'I haven't the least idea.'

'He's come to meet her—and in a nice line in cars, too. And brand new. I bet that lightened the load in his wallet. Don't you know anything about her?'

'I know everything about her. The island of Jersey is some—'

'Yes, yes, yes; we went into that.'

'—fifty or sixty square miles, which means that gossip can't spread very far; it can only—'

'So what do you know about her?'

'She's the only child of one of Jersey's overlords; thirteenth century manor and the rights that go with it and thick walls and very small windows. Father very rich, very old, very touchy. Daughter very rebellious. The two of them disagree.'

'Over money?'

'Over men. She believes that they love her for herself; Father's convinced that they're after his money. The latest rumour says that she got engaged without his consent; if so, it was probably to the fellow over there with the green car; if so, I hope not because he doesn't look as though he could handle her.'

'What's her name?'

'De Vrais. Old Jersey name. Jessica de Vrais. Where are you going?'

14

'He seems to have gone off to see about her luggage. This is my chance to find out what her views are on talking to strangers.'

'Look,' pointed out Joss, 'you made me take this holiday. You insisted on doing the trip now instead of in June, as I suggested. You persuaded me to—'

'I'll be back in a minute. I haven't been hanging round here just waiting for you to arrive; I've done everything I could to get Betsy unloaded. I've worked like a horse. I've stepped on to soap boxes and argued with the strikers, fluently but unsuccessfully. I've done everything short of actually taking the ship apart and yanking the car out. I hate to say we're ditched, but we are and that's final. We've got to think of something. You start thinking; I'll be back.'

Joss merely nodded and watched him walk away; he was well accustomed to Sebastian's swift approaches and strategic retreats. A glance round the quay showed no sign of Maurice, so without impatience he strolled to a nearby bench and sat down to watch the confused scene. Harassed officials hurried by, pursued by travellers anxious to learn the latest developments in the strike situation. Porters looked for straying clients, failed to find them and left their luggage in piles on the jetty while they searched farther afield. A long queue waited to make telephone calls; loud-speakers blared advice and admonition and pleaded for order. Out in the roadway, the confusion was if anything worse. Buses came and went; ancient coaches, pressed into service, drove up empty and in an incredibly short time drove away again filled to capacity. Round the few remaining taxis, shouting groups drove bargains with drivers; prices mounted to fantastic figures and still people clambered in, crowded to suffocation, and were taken off to the sound of angry shouts from those left behind.

Maurice's small form appeared for a moment, vanished in the crowd and reappeared again close to Joss.

'Nobody,' he announced briefly.

'You mean you didn't see them?' asked Joss.

'I looked from there to there.' Maurice's arms made a wide sweep. 'They weren't anywhere. Where are they?'

'They'll be here soon; there's no hurry,' said Joss.

His tone was untroubled, but a slight uneasiness was creeping over him. He had undertaken the charge lightly: he was to see that the child, with his wicker suitcase, was transferred from the boat to the care of his aunt and grandfather, who would be awaiting him. No more. The mother had said nothing about keeping an eye on the child on the journey, or upon arrival. This, mused Joss, was just as well; handing over was one thing—anybody could hand over—but it would take a keen eye to follow all the movements of this supercharged and hell-bent infant. More than once, on the way over, he had seen the small figure the centre of outraged adults all clamouring to know who was in charge of him. Joss had not claimed the privilege.

Coming out of his reverie and looking round to locate Maurice, Joss saw to his dismay that there would soon be a repetition of the angry scenes on board. The boy, filling in time while awaiting his relations, had applied himself to scratching his initials on pieces of unclaimed or unattended luggage belonging to those who, by reason of the strike, were busy elsewhere. Joss, with a stern effort, overcame his impulse to interfere; tempers were strained enough as it was, and he had no desire to find himself arguing with the owners of the cases. Moreover, his knowledge of small boys, though not extensive, was enough to convince him that carving initials on handy objects was one of their less dangerous pursuits. A boy as active as this one, he reflected, a boy, above all, who was the owner of a businesslike penknife like that one, had to have some outlet; dam up this comparatively harmless channel and he'd probably cause real trouble. If people didn't want strangers' names engraved on their property, they should keep a sharper eye on it.

He looked across to where Sebastian now stood talking to Jessica de Vrais. A fast worker, Sebastian, he mused, by no means for the first time. Fast, and successful. If he himself had strolled across and spoken to her, she would no doubt have summoned a policeman—and this despite the fact that he looked considerably more harmless than Sebastian.

He brooded for some time on the vagaries of women. Kittle cattle. You never knew what went on in their minds, or even if they had minds. Perhaps it was his own fault; bad approach or slow follow-up. He was fairly young, he was not repulsive-looking, his health was good and he had a good job. You'd think a woman would find enough there to start on, but perhaps his tentative attempts made them—

With a jerk, his attention came back to Maurice—but not soon enough. That artist had moved by imperceptible degrees nearer to the property of Joss and Sebastian; he had carved his name fancifully upon Joss's Gladstone bag; Sebastian's expensive zip-fastening case bore the impression Maurice Pierre Carron. Now he was working on the largest of the beautiful, matching set of luggage arrayed near Jessica de Vrais.

For one instant Joss fought his longing to take swift retributory action. This, then, was the reason Master Carron's luggage was of wicker. He glanced uneasily towards Jessica; Sebastian had left her and she was looking in this direction, but from where she stood, she could not detect the damage. It would be sensible to move; if her temper was anything like her father's, he would not like to be at hand when she next laid eyes on her suitcase.

Taking Maurice's hand in a firm grip, he drew him away into the crowd and threaded his way to the road to see whether there was any sign of an agitated grandfather or aunt. Nobody, however, seemed anxious to claim the boy. It was not to be wondered at, thought Joss; perhaps they had property to protect. But all the same, he couldn't keep the boy indefinitely. He frowned uneasily; he had no idea how far the child's relations had to travel in order to reach St Malo, but if they had been coming by train—

'You see?' Maurice looked up at him. 'They aren't here.'

'No. There's no need to worry.'

'I'm not worried,' said Maurice in surprise. 'I'm glad, that's all.'

'What are you glad about?'

'I like it here. It's got trains. Why don't the trains go?'

'There's a strike. The drivers don't want to drive them.'

He answered absently Maurice's demand for more detailed explanation. He had become convinced that the boy's relations had been prevented by the strike from coming to meet him, and he was trying to remember the mother's instructions in Jersey: in the unlikely

19

event of there being nobody waiting for the boat, he was to—what was he to do? Joss wished that he had paid greater attention, but the idea of a hitch had not occurred to him. He remembered writing down something—a number, a telephone number. He had scribbled it down. Where?

He saw Jessica de Vrais moving with her escort towards the green car; taking Maurice by the hand, Joss went back to the bench and, sitting down, took a small diary from his pocket and began ruffling swiftly through its pages. He was absorbed in the task when he heard Sebastian's angry voice.

'Who the hell—Look at that!'

'Yes.' Joss spoke absently. 'I saw. C— D—E—'

'But you can't have seen this! Look what that son of Satan's done to the luggage! Look at it! Maurice Pierre something.'

'Carron,' supplied Joss. 'J—K—'

'Why didn't you stop him?' demanded Sebastian. 'You're in charge of him, aren't you?'

'No,' said Joss. 'No, I don't think I am. N—O—'

'If you're not, who is? If you are, then you ought to be keeping an eye on what he's doing. If you're not ... well, obviously somebody ought to be. Hasn't he got any relations?'

'All I said was that I'd hand him over.'

'Hand him over to whom?'

'To whoever came to fetch him.'

'Well, who's coming to fetch him?'

They looked at Maurice, who was sitting beside Joss. He appeared unmoved by the fact that his artistic efforts had met with neither appreciation nor approval; he also seemed uninterested in the discussion about his relations. All his energies were being directed to the effort of loosening one of his front teeth.

'I don't know who's coming, exactly,' said Joss. 'His—'

'My grandfather,' broke in Maurice, and gave a tentative tug to the tooth. 'He always comes with Tante Francine, except when he doesn't feel well. Then she comes. Tante Francine comes by herself. When will they come?'

'I don't know,' said Joss. 'Soon. If only I could find—'

'What are you looking for?' enquired Sebastian.

'The telephone number.'

'Grandfather's?'

'No. There's no phone at the house. If you want to get hold of them, you have to ring up this other number I'm looking for.'

'There isn't any telephone in their house,' explained Maurice. 'Tante Francine says it would be too much money. She—'

'Never mind about Tante Francine,' said Sebastian. 'Now, Joss, let's get it straight. You had to hand him over; if nobody was waiting

21

for him, you had to telephone to somebody whose number you can't find. Right?'

'I come every year,' Maurice informed them. 'I come in September and they come to meet me. Tante Francine—'

'Quiet,' ordered Sebastian. '*Tais-toi.* In other words, pipe down. Well, Joss?'

'I'll probably come across the number in a minute,' said Joss, still searching. 'I'm certain I wrote it down.'

'If it isn't their own phone,' said Sebastian, 'it must belong to someone who takes messages for them. Maurice, whose telephone does your grandfather use?'

'Madame Seyboule's,' said Maurice promptly.

'Then all we have to do,' pointed out Sebastian, 'is look up the number of this Madame Seyboule in the appropriate directory and ask her—'

'But that's the trouble,' said Joss. 'The telephone isn't in her name either; don't ask me why. Now I can see why there was so much fuss about making me take down the number. I think I may have written it on an odd piece of paper.'

'Here's a bit of paper.' Sebastian plucked it from between the leaves of the diary. 'This it?'

'No.' Joss examined the paper and his frown deepened. 'But I could have sworn I'd torn up this—'

'—but you tore up the telephone number

22

instead. Well that,' said Sebastian, 'tears everything up. What do we do now?'

'We don't know whether they were coming by train. Maurice,' asked Joss, 'does your grandfather come by car?'

'No. He wants one,' said Maurice, 'but Tante Francine says—'

'Tante Francine again. That woman keeps coming up,' said Sebastian. 'Look, Joss, I'm going over to the A.A. to get a final word about how much chance there is of getting Betsy ashore. You take young what's-his-name—'

'Maurice Pierre Carron,' said Maurice.

'As if I didn't know,' said Sebastian bitterly. 'Take him into a clearing, if you can find one, Joss, and walk him up and down in full view. Perhaps they're here and haven't seen him yet in this confusion. See you soon.'

He walked away. Joss, with Maurice hopping beside him, walked up and down the road. When Maurice was claimed, he reflected, he and Sebastian would have to settle something; they could not wait about here aimlessly waiting for the strike to come to an end. It was the worst of luck, but perhaps they could salvage something; perhaps they could enjoy a less mobile holiday. They could—

He came to himself to find that Maurice was no longer by his side; instead, an elderly woman had come into the road from the quay and was standing blocking his way. He looked down at her in surprise and was about to step

23

out of her path when he found that Sebastian had joined him and was speaking firmly to the stranger.

'No, madame, it is quite impossible to help you. As you guessed, we are not able to get our car off the ship. Come on, Joss.'

'Wait. Please pay attention,' commanded the woman.

Joss looked at her, and his survey took in details that had escaped Sebastian. He saw a tall, gaunt figure whose appearance he described to himself as ramshackle. She wore a shapeless black hat over fuzzy white hair, a dusty black coat and a far-from-clean black dress. Her feet were encased in black suede boots, elastic-sided, bald with age. She gave, at first glance, a general impression of shabbiness, but Joss, looking more closely, saw here and there items of startling incongruity: the gleam of gold at her wrists, the flash of diamonds upon her bosom. He noted also the complete assurance of her manner, her self-confidence, the air of command in her bearing. Her sharp tones held authority; the hard, unwavering look she was directing at him showed her to be of no disposition to brook contradiction. And like Sebastian, he was impressed most of all by her nose, with its suggestion of disdain, of hauteur.

She lifted a beringed, begrimed finger and waggled it at Joss.

'I am the Comtesse de Chandillot,' she

informed him. 'We are all in a little fix, no?'

'There is,' admitted the fascinated Joss, 'a temporary check.'

'It is impossible that you and your friend get your car. I have enquired. The strike will go on. The car will go in the ship back to England, and what will you do? You do not wish to go back with it?'

The question was rhetorical; there was obviously a proposition on the way, and Joss thought that he could anticipate it.

'You want us,' he said, 'to share a taxi with you?'

The small black eyes narrowed in displeasure.

'If you wait, I shall say what I want, so please pay attention. You see that taxi over there?'

Both men turned to inspect it. They saw near them a high black vehicle, hearselike, dust-covered, mud-streaked. The garages of St Malo had been swept to provide, at great cost, transport for the stranded; this was the last of the sweepings. It had been—perhaps, estimated Joss, at the turn of the century—a car of note; as with the old woman in black, something of vanished elegance could be glimpsed beneath the overlying seediness, but it looked more suitable for exhibition in a museum than for present day use.

They turned from wondering contemplation, and Sebastian spoke.

'You've hired that thing?' he asked in

amazement.

'It is mine. I have bought it,' said the Comtesse.

There was a pause; she waited for comment, but Joss and Sebastian could say nothing they felt to be adequate.

'You have no car,' went on the Comtesse, 'because it is shut up and you will not get it out. I have this car, which is old but good—but there is nobody to drive it.' The men glanced at the taxi driver and she gave a snort of contempt. 'Pff! You think that I would go with that mistake of a man? By no means. Which is more, he would rob me before we had gone a dozen kilometres. No, for heaven's sake. But if you will drive me, I will pay you well. My chateau is near Lysaine—that is perhaps two hundred kilometres from here, no more. We shall be there soon. From there you may do as you wish; if you wish to go on by train, and if then the trains are going, you can go. If you wish to stay for a week, two weeks in my chateau, you may do so, but in this case I will not pay you any money. I wish to leave this place at once; I have said that I have urgent business, and I will not be kept here simply because a lot of dirty Communists wish to keep me.' She saw Sebastian about to speak, and held up a hand. 'Please pay attention. I am going for the present with this old misery of a man; there are papers which I must sign. When I come back, we shall go at once. If you stay

26

here, what can you do? The hotels are all full. The taxis have all been taken. There are no more coaches and it will be long before arrangements are made for those who are without transport. If you think of all this, you will see that I am right.'

Without further words, she turned and walked to the taxi driver. He fell into step two respectful paces behind her and the two figures disappeared round a corner of the dock buildings. Sebastian came out of a daze and turned to face Joss.

'Did I stand here and let that hag order me about?' he asked.

'A hag, but bejewelled,' said Joss thoughtfully. 'What place was that that Coleridge mentioned? You know—

And rags, and hags, and hideous wenches;
I counted two and seventy stenches.'

'I don't know and I don't care,' said Sebastian. 'This is no time to start quoting.'

'What do we do?' asked Joss. 'Do we go with her?'

Sebastian stared at him in surprise.

'Go driving round the countryside with a bogus comtesse in that ... that hearse?'

'My guess,' said Joss, 'is that her claim to the title is valid. Joining up with her might be interesting. The alternatives aren't.'

'What alternatives?'

'Well—' Joss enumerated on long, bony fingers—'we could go back to England with Betsy and do a tour of thc Lake District.'

'To hell with the Lake District,' said Sebastian.

'Or Wales.'

'To hell with Wales.'

'Or we could take a bus and make our way to Brittany—Quimper, for example—and—'

'—go round the Potteries? To hell with Potteries. Besides, we've seen them.'

'Or we could stow our suitcases somewhere and take bare essentials and hitchhike and—To hell with hitchhiking?'

'Yes.'

'Or we could accept the Comtesse's proposition and get (a) the fun, if any; (b) some foreign currency if you're not too proud to accept it; (c) transport, of a kind. I'll do what you like, of course, but if you want me to state a preference, I'm all for driving the old lady. What about you?'

'I suppose so,' agreed Sebastian moodily. 'Well, if we're going, hadn't you better do something about finding young Maurice's relations? If they don't come, we can't go. Isn't there any sign of them anywhere?'

'Nobody's claimed him.'

'I don't wonder. Well, assuming that they're stuck somewhere, how about finding out where he lives and seeing if we can't deliver him? Grandfather might live on the route to this

28

place the Comtesse mentioned, Lysaine, and we'd have a reasonable chance of getting there before they've had a chance to set off. We've got a car—if you call it a car—and they're probably arguing about how they're going to get here. Where does he live? Hey, Maurice! Where is he?'

It was some time before they found him; then they stood beside the telegraph pole and summarily ordered him down. He descended with agility and smiled a toothless and triumphant smile.

'Good Lord, he's pulled out a tooth!' said Joss.

'Never mind his tooth. Maurice, where does your grandfather live?'

'At Cloisy,' said Maurice. 'His house is called *Marielle*, because that was what my grandmother's name was before she died. When she died, Tante Francine went—'

'All right, that's all for the moment,' said Sebastian. 'There's a map with those car documents, Joss; get it out, will you?'

They bent over a map, studying it.

'Can't see any Cloisy within the two-hundred-kilometre radius,' said Sebastian at last. 'Maurice, whereabouts is this Cloisy?'

'You go in a train and then you get there,' said Maurice helpfully.

'Here comes the Comtesse,' said Joss.

The Comtesse came up to them impatiently.

'Why is not everything ready?' she enquired.

29

'Why do we not go?'

'Hitch, Comtesse,' explained Sebastian. 'We're waiting for this little boy's relations.'

'Why should we wait? Who is the child?' demanded the Comtesse.

'Maurice Pierre Carron,' said Maurice.

'We can't go until we've handed him over to his grandfather or his aunt,' explained Joss. 'They were to have met him here, but they're probably held up by the strike. We were just trying to find out if he lived anywhere on the way to—'

'If you give him to the police,' broke in the Comtesse, 'they will arrange everything. Come, let us go.'

'Hold on, Comtesse,' said Sebastian. 'We can't just—'

'Is he your kinsman?' asked the Comtesse.

'My—? No, he isn't,' disclaimed Sebastian. 'But we can't just walk off the quay and abandon him. Somewhere, searching for him, there's Grandpère and Tante Francine. They live at a place called ... called what, Maurice?'

'Cloisy.'

The Comtesse stared at him.

'Cloisy?' she repeated in astonishment. 'Cloisy? The Cloisy which is near Salvan?'

'I haven't the faintest idea,' said Sebastian.

'Yes,' said Maurice.

'You mean—' began Sebastian.

'Come, come, come,' broke in the Comtesse impatiently. 'Let us go. Bring the child.'

'Bring the ... you mean he lives somewhere near you?' asked Joss.

'Of course, of course. Should we take him if he lived, for instance, in Africa? Cloisy, Lysaine; Lysaine, Cloisy; it's all the same, don't you see?'

'No, I don't see,' said Sebastian.

'You live near Cloisy?' Maurice asked the Comtesse.

'Never mind where I live,' she answered. 'I can go to where I live without any assistance from you, but you cannot reach your grandfather, who should be here to meet you, unless I take you with me. So come. Why do we stand about? Some people are more slow than others to understand what is said to them, but now that I have explained that Cloisy is Lysaine, we need not wait any more. If you will put the luggage into the car, I will go to the police and tell them that we are taking the child Carron to his home at Cloisy; if his relations come, they will be informed. I have not heard of any Carrons at Cloisy, but if they live there, they will not need to be told who I am. Please to be ready when I return.'

When she returned, they were ready. Sebastian spent the time gazing incredulously into the car's engine. Joss had fetched a porter and had begun to direct the loading of the luggage, and then gave in to Maurice's pleas to be allowed to do it.

'Sure you can manage?' asked Joss.

'Yes, of course I can. Please let me!'

Joss applied himself to dusting the seats at the back of the car; the accumulation of years rose and choked him.

'Keep an eye on Maurice,' he called to Sebastian. 'If he claims every piece of luggage he carved his name on, we'll find ourselves with a lot more stuff than we set out with.'

There was no response from the absorbed Sebastian. Joss sneezed, dusted and sneezed again. By the time the Comtesse returned, he had achieved a fair degree of cleanliness; he gave a final flick of the duster, assisted the Comtesse to mount the high running board and saw her comfortably disposed against the cushions. Oblivious to her protests, he shut Maurice in with her and went to the front and climbed up beside Sebastian and took the wheel. A glass partition separated them, to their relief, from the passengers at the back.

The huge car drew away from the quay. The noise of shouting and argument was left behind. The last group of strikers, the last stranded travellers receded. Behind them was St Malo; also behind them, Sebastian remembered with a pang, was Betsy, trapped in the dark hold. Somewhere, probably between them and Paris, was Jessica de Vrais in the graceful green car.

In front of them was all France.

CHAPTER TWO

Jessica de Vrais was twenty-two, the only child of an elderly and irritable widower. Their life together had not been harmonious. During Jessica's schooling, first in England and later in Switzerland, Mr de Vrais had enjoyed some years of intermittent peace, but when his daughter came home from her finishing school and settled down at home, the sleeping feud between them sprang to life.

Though they thought alike on almost all matters, they agreed on none; least of all did they see eye to eye on the subject of men. Jessica, pretty and popular, invited them to come and stay; Mr de Vrais, irritable and suspicious, invited them to go away and stay away. Fortune-hunters all, he said furiously to his daughter. One and all, they were after her money—his money. One look, he shouted, and he could smell them a mile off. Hangers-on. Yahoos. Parasites.

When Jessica, at the end of June, announced that she was engaged to one of them—a young Frenchman named Hubert Ramage whom she had known for little more than two weeks—Mr de Vrais granted to the suitor a short interview and at the end of it announced that any further communication between the couple would be made over his dead body.

Jessica, for once, said nothing. When Hubert went back to France, she showed no sign of regret. But on a cool September morning she rose early, left a conclusive little note for her father, carried her suitcases down to the car and drove into St Helier to catch the boat to St Malo. When her father read the note, it said, she would be married to Hubert.

Almost as soon as the boat drew away from the pier at Jersey, she found herself regretting her action. Lonely, miserable, homesick and seasick, she thought of her father with unaccustomed tolerance and of Hubert with apprehension. He would be at St Malo, waiting, he had said. He would marry her and cherish her, he had declared. But she was not her father's daughter for nothing; she had his shrewdness, his sound common sense, and there were one or two things about Hubert which, almost against her will, had impressed themselves disagreeably upon her. She did not know him very well. He might be all she hoped, or he might not. She had made preparations for either eventuality.

She crept up on deck as the ship neared St Malo; the approach of land had cured her of her seasickness and she moved cautiously now only because she meant to station herself in a position from which she could see Hubert without being seen by him. One look, and she would know.

But after one look, she was still uncertain.

He looked even more handsome, more debonair here in a neat brown suit than he had looked in bathing trunks in Jersey in June. He looked, at this distance, thoroughly reliable. And the car ... yes, the car killed instantaneously all the qualms her father had communicated to her regarding the disinterestedness of his suit. She knew the make of the car and she knew its price. If Hubert owned that, if it was his and he had paid for it, there was no need for him to hunt for a fortune; he was standing beside one.

She went below feeling almost happy. When she came down the gangway carrying the smallest piece of her expensive and matching set of luggage, she looked cool and assured, demure and appealing all at once. She allowed Hubert to kiss her hand and then her cheek; she wished that the touch of his lips had raised a warmer response in her breast, but remembered that a quay was not, perhaps, a place for emotion.

'My darling, I have waited for you,' declared Hubert, 'for so long.'

Jessica was about to ask whether the boat had docked later than was expected when she saw his ardent expression and checked herself. She let her gaze rest with not too much interest upon the car, and he smiled proudly.

'It is yours. I bought it for you,' he said.

'Oh Hubert, did you honestly?' she said warmly, and wished she had chosen a happier adverb. 'It looks … I think it's—'

'It goes very fast,' said Hubert. 'I am taking you to Paris, to some friends of mine: René and Carla Roche. Carla will look after you until we are married. Everything is arranged. I have—'

'Just a moment, Hubert; there's my luggage.'

'I will see to it,' said Hubert. 'From this time, you must leave everything to me.'

'Yes,' agreed Jessica. 'But I think I'll see the things through the Customs first. You wait here. Will this strike,' she asked over her shoulder as she went, 'make any difference to us?'

'Not in the least,' said Hubert with confidence. 'It is only for the railway travellers; it does not affect us at all.'

Jessica, not gifted with second sight, believed this implicitly and followed her porter to the Customs shed. He prepared to lay her luggage on the counter and Jessica put out a restraining hand.

'Not there,' she said. 'Wait.'

She ran her eyes down the line of Customs officials, studying each one intently. Having chosen the one best suited to her purposes, she beckoned to the porter.

'Over there,' she said.

She stood beside the cases, her heart beginning to beat fast. Her outward bearing, however, was cool and quiet. She looked exactly what she was: rich, leisured, well

36

brought-up, poised.

The Customs officer—young and susceptible-looking—came up to her; she looked at him with gentle expectation and appeared not to hear his hint that she might have something to declare. Her hands hovered over the cases, ready to open them at his command.

'This one, please,' he requested, pointing to the largest of the set.

The case was unlocked. Jessica turned the clasps, snapped them open, raised the lid slowly and waited.

To right and left, there was a sudden hush. Heads turned, voices murmured gently, those standing near closed in to get a better view.

'Ah!' said an old man standing beside Jessica. 'It is ... it is yours?'

'Mine, yes,' said Jessica, and gave him a small, shy smile.

Nobody spoke for some moments; everybody was gazing at the pure white foam of tulle that lay exposed to view in the suitcase. Yard upon yard, tenderly folded; even as they looked, the delicate fabric seemed to be rising, billowing. In the centre, gently laid upon the topmost fold, rested a small circlet of orange blossom.

The onlookers fell into a tender reverie; for a few moments it was as though organ notes filled the air. Then there was a general sigh and the strike, which had receded, returned, and with it, mundane matters. The Customs official closed the top of the case, marked it and its fellows as cleared and turned regretfully to the next traveller. Jessica's porter gathered up her luggage and she went out to join Hubert and accompany him to Paris.

Hubert, however, was not quite ready to go; he would telephone, he said, to see where they could get lunch; the strike had made a delay and it was almost time for the meal. Did Jessica, he asked, want to come with him to make the arrangements?

Jessica said that she would wait near the car. Her voice was a little absent, for she had observed, a short distance away, signs with which she was only too familiar: a man, a good-looking man, measuring her and finding the measurements exact. In the brief, cool look she sent him, she gathered all she wanted to know: he was about thirty-three or -four, attractive, and only too clearly aware of the fact. It would be a pleasure to knock the supports from under him.

He approached, as she had known he would. He came unhesitatingly and with well-feigned surprise.

'It's Jessica!' he exclaimed as he came up to her. 'Jessica de Vrais! What on earth are you doing here?'

'Being picked up by strange men,' said Jessica calmly. 'My fiancé will be back in a moment.'

'That's too long to leave you about,' said Sebastian reproachfully. 'If by any chance he isn't able to drive you—'

'We're leaving for Paris very soon,' said Jessica. 'Please don't let me keep you.'

'You're treading on a fallen man,' Sebastian said. 'My car's down in the hold of the Southampton boat, strikebound. My trip's gone to blazes.'

'I'm sorry,' said Jessica, and meant it. 'What are you going to do?'

'What do you suggest?'

'In your place, I think I'd go back to England and go on a nice tour of Devon or Cornwall.'

'You don't think the excitement would prove fatal?'

'It might,' said Jessica, and there was a note of hope in her voice.

'I know Paris fairly well,' said Sebastian. 'What part did you say you and your fiancé—'

'I'm sorry about your car,' Jessica broke in firmly. 'It must be maddening to have your holiday spoilt. But our car, as you see, is a two seater.'

'And there isn't the slightest chance that your fiancé—'

'—will suddenly become indisposed? Not the smallest. Good-bye.'

'You mean every word?'

'Every word.'

'Well, it's been a pleasure,' said Sebastian

39

with obvious sincerity.

'How,' enquired Jessica as he turned away, 'did you know my name?'

'A sort of instinct. In addition to which, the man you see over there, Joss Armstrong by name, is a friend of mine; he was, in fact, coming on this abortive trip with me. He lives in, or on, Jersey; he's got an accountant's job there. He—'

'—gave you my dossier.'

'There were serious omissions, and I wanted to fill them in. He only told me—'

'Well?'

'It doesn't matter. Whenever I meet a lovely girl,' said Sebastian, 'I meet her too late. Good-bye.'

'Good-bye,' said Jessica, and watched him walk away.

Hubert, returning, reported that the Hotel de l'Univers had agreed, after pressure and persuasion, to reserve a table for lunch.

'There are many stranded travellers,' he explained. 'It is rather early for lunch, but it is the only time they can arrange. It is better to have a good lunch now than a·bad one later. Shall we go?'

When they returned to the quay after the meal, Jessica was feeling a good deal better, and Hubert was looking a little dazed. She had eaten a dozen escargots and a dozen good-sized shrimps; after these preliminaries she had put away an escalope of veal and potatoes and

40

vegetables and three rum babas and some extremely strong cheese; all these had been very expensively washed down, but the money, he thought, had on the whole been worth it for the steady mellowing of mood which had accompanied her enjoyment of the meal. His self-confidence, which had been ebbing, revived. All would be well. He had scarcely dared to hope that his plans would go through, but here they were, it was clear, going through without a hitch.

The hitch was soon to occur, and it proved a serious one: a piece of Jessica's luggage was missing, the largest of the matching group. The porter who had been left in charge stated that he had placed it with the other pieces near the Customs shed, together with that of other passengers. Someone, clearly, had removed it with their own luggage; whether by accident or by intent it was not for him to say.

It took time to search the quay, the sheds, even the crowded roadway; there was no sign of the case. Hubert, doing his best to follow all the suggestions offered by helpful bystanders, caught sight of Jessica's face and was surprised at its pallor. Her voice, as she questioned officials, held an oddly desperate note.

'Did it ... was there anything of great value in it?' he asked at last.

She looked at him, panic showing clearly in her eyes.

'Yes, there was. I mean ... yes. My wedding

dress was in it.'

'Your ... oh,' said Hubert. 'I see. Your wedding dress. Then at all costs it must be found.'

A shabby old man leaning against a wall supplied the first clue. He had seen such a piece of baggage, he stated, being put on to a taxi. No more was forthcoming; his memory, he said, had failed. Hubert revived it with some money, but the process had to be repeated several times before the man told all he knew. Jessica, looking on impatiently, was reminded of a dog barking for scraps. The final story, however, sounded convincing: Marcel Deroux had sold his taxi to an old lady; the old lady had gone away in it, taking with her two Englishmen, one Jersey-French boy and the missing piece of luggage.

'I saw her. I remember her,' said Jessica to Hubert.

'The old lady?'

'Yes. You must have seen her, Hubert. She was walking about the quay dressed in terrible black clothes ... like black sacks.'

Hubert had seen her. He had, in fact, seen her twice—but seeing, he had refused to believe. One could, he told himself, suffer from hallucinations. One could, in moments of excitement, see things, persons, horrors which were not there. One could even imagine on the quay that large, black-clad form...

The first time, he had averted his eyes; when

42

he looked again, the form had vanished. Weak with relief, he had smiled at himself for letting his imagination run away with him. A person, even that person, could not be in two places at once. She was in London; *enfin*, she could not be at St Malo.

The second glimpse, a closer one, had shaken him so much that he had retired to the car, pulled his hat low over his eyes, crouched in the seat and counted up to forty. At forty-one, peering out cautiously, he had seen no sign of the dreaded figure; after reflection, he convinced himself that even if it were she, even if by a miracle, or by mischance, she were here, he had no reason to be afraid. She would not dream that he could be at St Malo in this magnificent car. Catching sight of him, she would tell herself that it was but a strong likeness; she would be surprised, for men who combined good looks, elegance and *je-ne-sais-quoi* were not, after all, to be seen every day. No! There was no danger. He had but to keep his hat pulled low, so, and take care to see before being seen.

'I do not,' he told Jessica firmly, 'notice old women in old black sacks.'

'We can trace her,' said Jessica. 'We'll have to find this Deroux; he can tell us where she went.'

Deroux, to Hubert's relief, was not easy to find, but Jessica displayed a persistence that surprised and dismayed him. She located the man at last at his home, sleeping off his lunch. But though only half-awake when questioned by Jessica, he had no difficulty in remembering the old lady, her name and her destination.

'Her name, mademoiselle,' he said, beginning at the beginning, 'was—'

'Where was she going?' broke in Jessica. 'Her destination—what was it?'

'She was going to the Chateau de Chandillot, mademoiselle. It is near Lysaine; I heard her say this to the Englishmen who were to drive her. She was in a hurry to get there. It is her home. She is the Comtesse de Chandillot.'

Jessica drew a long breath of relief. The colour returned to her cheeks and she turned swiftly to Hubert.

'Lysaine. Have you ever heard of it?' she asked.

'Yes. Perhaps.' Hubert seemed to pause and swallow with difficulty. 'Lysaine, yes.'

'How far away is it?' asked Jessica eagerly.

'It is ... oh, it is very far. It is two hundred kilometres, at least. At least that. If not much more,' said Hubert.

'That's no distance,' said Jessica. 'We can do that on our heads in that car. Let's go.'

'But they are there by now. It is useless to follow,' said Hubert hurriedly.

'Why? We've got a car that can catch up anything on the road and—'

'Oh, no, no. No, I am sure we could not,' said Hubert.

44

'But ...' She turned to stare at him. 'We could at least try. They must have stopped somewhere for lunch, and we can—'

'But that is just it.' Hubert clutched eagerly at this straw. 'We should miss them, don't you see?'

'No, I don't see.' Jessica's voice was cool. 'Even if we did, we could go to the chateau and find them there.'

'Why should we not telephone?' suggested Hubert. 'She would send back the case. Or she could send it to Paris. Yes, she could send it to Paris; that will be the best arrangement.'

She turned to study him. To her surprise and dismay, he seemed in the last few moments to have taken on a new and infinitely less pleasing personality. He even appeared to have shrunk. He no longer looked handsome; he no longer appeared debonair. His self-confidence had vanished, had been ripped off like a mask, leaving exposed a very young, very pale and very frightened man.

'What in the world—What's the matter, Hubert?' asked Jessica anxiously. 'You look ... you don't look very well, or something.'

'I'm fine, fine,' Hubert assured her nervously. 'Perhaps a little tired from driving here so fast; nothing more.'

'Well, you don't need to drive to this chateau,' said Jessica, sympathy in her voice. 'I'll drive. We can get there and pick up my—'

'No, no,' said Hubert. 'That would not be a
45

good idea.'

Impatience crept into her voice.

'But ... I don't understand,' she said. 'My suitcase, with my wedding dress in it, gets lost. We look for it. We find it. There's no possibility that this man's mistaken; he even described the blue label on the case. How could he do that if he hadn't actually seen it? Nobody told him anything about a blue label. So if the case, which I must have, is somewhere on the road between here and this place called Lysaine, or if it's in the chateau de whatever it was, what's wrong with driving down there to get it back? They won't know how to send it to me. They won't even know where to send it.'

'It is so far out of our way,' pleaded Hubert.

'No, it isn't. And how can I arrive in Paris without my wedding dress?'

'We shall get another,' Hubert promised her, and saw the de Vrais temper flash suddenly into her eyes. Uneasily, he thought of old Mr de Vrais, whose temper, though violent, he had not greatly feared, but whose perspicacity he had found disconcerting.

'You,' said Jessica, with dangerous calm, 'can make what arrangements you please. I am going to find this Comtesse de—de—What was the name?' she asked the taxi driver.

'Her name was de Chandillot, mademoiselle. The Comtesse de Chandillot. She was tall; about so tall, with—'

'Never mind about all that.' Jessica turned

46

to confront Hubert. 'I'm going, Hubert, whether you come or not,' she told him, 'and for the life of me I can't imagine why you're raising all these objections. Are you coming with me or aren't you?'

'I ... please consider,' begged Hubert. 'You are here, and we are going to Paris, and everything is arranged with René and Carla. We can get another dress for you. What is a dress, after all? We can get many. Come, I beg you, and put away this idea of meeting this dreadful old woman. Let us—'

'Dreadful old ...' Jessica's eyes narrowed thoughtfully. 'You know her?'

'No. Yes. Perhaps,' said Hubert. 'I have heard of her. You would not at all care for her, I assure you.'

She scarcely heard him. She was thinking clearly at last, and with all her father's acumen. This, she realized, was not the self-possessed man in whose hands she had been prepared ... well, almost prepared to place her future. This was a thin and pale and perspiring young man who looked ... yes, he did; he looked terrified. Something had happened in the last few minutes; something about this Comtesse had frightened him badly.

Small, unrelated matters floated into her mind and assembled themselves into a reasonably clear and far from reassuring picture. Her father had stated that Hubert had not a penny of his own; in the heat of

47

contradicting him, she had omitted to remember that Mr de Vrais often spoke in anger, but seldom or never spoke without the book; her failure to catch him out, indeed, had been one of the most maddening features of their relationship. If he said that Hubert hadn't a penny, she ought to have known that he was speaking after shrewd and exhaustive enquiry. And if Hubert hadn't a penny, how had he managed to meet her at St Malo with a new, shatteringly expensive car? And why had he concealed his knowledge of this Comtesse, and why was he so firmly opposed to following her ... facing her? Why ... But wait a minute. Jessica knitted her brows and fished deep for other facts. In a moment she had drawn up a heavy catch.

'Why ...' She stared at Hubert. 'Your name,' she said slowly.

'Purely coincidence,' said Hubert promptly.

'You told me,' went on Jessica, unheeding, 'that your name was Hubert Leonardo Rimbault de Chandillot Ramage. And this Comtesse—'

'There are de Chandillots here, there, everywhere,' said Hubert. 'They are like the Smiths and the Joneses. They—'

'You told me that your grandmother was dead.'

'My grandmother? Certainly my grandmother is dead. I told you the truth. She died many, many years ago, in—'

'I don't care what she died in,' said Jessica unfeelingly. 'All I know is that this Comtesse is related to you and—'

'No, no, no, no!' disclaimed Hubert passionately. 'She is nothing to me. Nothing. Nothing at all. Nothing. Simply, my aunt.'

'Your aunt!'

'My aunt. Nothing more, this I assure you.'

'Your aunt! But you—'

'And now you see,' he went on rapidly, 'why it is that I know she is a dreadful old woman. Because she is. This is the truth, at least. She is—'

'And that car—' Jessica's eyes went to it contemptuously—'is hers.'

'Hers? But no!' There was conviction in his loud outcry; he sounded like a parent being dispossessed of an only child. 'Mine! It is mine! I paid for it!'

'Then it wasn't,' said Jessica in her father's own factual voice, 'your money.'

Hubert drew out a handkerchief and wiped his damp brow.

'Listen to me,' he begged. 'I can—' He paused, looked round at the circle of interested faces gathered about them and, taking Jessica's arm, drew her aside. 'I can explain everything. I can—'

'It was your aunt's money,' said Jessica.

'And so, in a way, mine.'

'You bought that car with her money.'

'I . . . in some way, yes. Perhaps. But let me

explain. I must tell you that she is old and rich and mean. She is so mean, please believe me, that she spends nothing. Nothing. There are people who are mean, who are misers, but she is—' the words poured out, swift, passionate and convincing—'she is of them all the meanest. If you saw her home—' he shuddered—'you would understand. It is terrible. She lives in the chateau, although it is mine by right, but she does not paint it, she does not repair it, she does not engage servants—only one man, a caretaker. She lives only in one room, and she does not spend money on food, on clothes, even on soap; you will believe me when I tell you that she is dirty; she does not wash. She does not wash herself or even her clothes. Only for one thing she lives: for her furniture. There, in the chateau, she keeps valuable, priceless pieces. They are not in the rooms for use, you understand? They are kept there as you would keep them in a warehouse. She buys them and she sells them. She buys them for less than they are worth; she finds them, it is said, by instinct, by smell. In places where nobody else would imagine to look, she finds beautiful old pieces; often they are owned by people who do not know their value, and she buys them for nothing and sells them for a fortune. She makes money, much money, nobody has been able to guess how much, but—'

'But I don't see what all this has to do—'

'Wait! I am about to tell you.' Hubert swept on. 'To me, her only kinsman; to me, who in justice should be her heir, she gives nothing. An allowance, a pittance which she can withhold at will. Work, she says to me. Earn, she says to me. Keep yourself, she says to me. But how? I ask her; how, tell me. And why? If she would let me live at the chateau, I could manage everything for her: engage the servants, beautify the rooms, repair what is rotting, make for her and for myself a life suitable to our name, our position. But the chateau is shut up, with only this old man in charge of it, while she goes here and there, to and fro, buying, buying, selling, selling, always at enormous profit. What she has amassed, nobody can say. And how much of it has she given me? Nothing. And in her will, what does she direct? That the furniture shall be mine? No. It will go to this and that museum. The chateau she cannot rob, for it is mine and—'

'But if it's yours, I don't see—'

'She turned me out. She says that I am of no use to anybody. And now she lives there, and how she lives! She does not change her clothes, she—'

'Hubert, you've said all that. I—'

'Wait, I am explaining. Would you not think that she would ask me, sometimes, to go and buy something which she has heard is to be sold? I know as much about valuable furniture as she does. Even she admits this. If she had

51

asked me to buy for her, I could have taken the opportunity to make something for myself. But she did not ask me. For years, she did not ask me. And then, without warning me, one day last week she sent for me and told me that I was to buy something. There was to be a sale in London and a sale in Paris. Both were on the same day; she could not go to both. So she gave me instructions to buy for her, at the Paris sale, a screen; very old, very beautiful. When I went to arrange with her, I thought that I would give her once more the opportunity to help me. I asked her for a better allowance. She refused.'

'But ... didn't you tell her you were going to be married?'

'Yes, I told her. But she said that she did not for a moment believe me. She said that I was inventing this story. She said that no girl but an idiot would agree to marry me; she does not care what she says to wound me. Then I asked her for money to keep me until I could ... to help me. She said to me, not one sou. And I was angry, you understand? I had to meet you, I had to make my arrangements, I had to have some money. And so I—'

'You needn't go on,' said Jessica coldly. 'You bought the car with the money she gave you for the screen.'

'Yes. No. It was,' protested Hubert, forgetting caution, 'only temporary. I would have paid it back as soon as ... I would have—'

He stopped, and there was a short silence

during which the position became completely clear to both: Jessica knew that he had intended to repay his aunt with her father's money; Hubert knew that she knew.

Hope died within him. He stared at her, misery overspreading his countenance, and then slowly, one by one, tears began to trickle down his cheeks. Jessica, scarlet with shame and embarrassment, glanced hurriedly round to see if anybody was looking.

Everybody was looking; some looked as though they were about to weep in sympathy. She waited for Hubert to wipe his eyes and then spoke to him in a cool but polite voice.

'Would you,' she asked, 'make one more attempt to find out whether by any chance the suitcase is here? The man may, after all, have been mistaken about the label; he may have invented the story. If your aunt went to London—'

'But the sale was yesterday. She could have returned.'

'It isn't likely, is it,' pointed out Jessica, 'that she'd leave immediately afterwards, on the night boat.'

'Anything at all is likely, especially if she found out that I had not bought the screen,' said Hubert mournfully.

'Well, would you ask once more at the Customs? The case may have turned up.'

'I will ask.' Hubert, unable to believe that things might yet be well, but willing to hope, turned and walked rapidly to the Customs shed, and Jessica, her face pale and expressionless, watched him go and for the first time sent up a heartfelt prayer of thankfulness for the cautious streak in her father's nature which had made him unwilling to take anything at its face value, which had given him eyes which bored holes through fakes and fortune-hunters and which on this occasion had bred in her sufficient distrust to cause her to make provision should anything go wrong with her plan of marrying Hubert. The plan had fallen with a crash on to the quay, but she had, thanks to her father, an alternative scheme, and now it must be put into operation.

But before this was possible, her suitcase must be found, and without delay.

There was nothing more to wait for. The car belonged to the Comtesse de Chandillot. The Comtesse should have it—in return for the suitcase.

With no further hesitation, Jessica turned and walked to the green car. She got in, and the bystanders, seeing her expression, parted hurriedly to give her passage. She switched on the engine, and a moment later the car shot forward and roared angrily on to the road and went rapidly out of sight.

Jessica, at the wheel, left Hubert behind and felt no pangs, either of regret or of remorse. Her thoughts were bitter, but they were directed not against Hubert but against fate.

She had asked, she considered, very little; all she had wanted was a man young enough, handsome enough and rich enough to prove to her father, once and for all, that his suspicions had been unfounded. A modest enough wish, but it had not been granted.

But there was no reason why Henry de Vrais should have the satisfaction of knowing that he had been right and she had been a fool. She was here in France, and she was not going home to be I-told-you-so'd. She was here, and for a time she was going to stay here. But she must find the suitcase. Once let her lay her hands on that, and all would be well. Caution would be rewarded; foresight would be repaid. She had, she told herself, nothing to fear.

Except, perhaps, the police.

CHAPTER THREE

The countryside between St Malo and Rennes does not rank scenically as the finest in France. There is nothing to catch the eye; the road is wide but unpicturesque, the villages unspectacular.

On this stretch of road, however, the attention of travellers is not usually on the scenery; tourists in cars starting out from St Malo are anxiously counting pieces of luggage or rearranging them to give more space and comfort to the occupants of the car; those nearing the port at the end of their tour are more often than not preoccupied with a multitude of details concerning papers and passports, the state of the sea and the hope of getting the contraband home without discovery. France, therefore, is content to reserve her beauties until visitors are at leisure to observe them. She awaits the seeing eye.

This was fortunate for Joss and Sebastian, for their first hour on the road was spent in trying to discover what the resurrected car had in mind, for it was only too clear, from the moment of leaving St Malo, that the vehicle had a mind, and a strong one. Like an old lady enjoying an outing after a long period of seclusion, the car seemed intoxicated by the new and extraordinary things to be seen on the road. She had been, in her day, a queen among cars, and so strong was her curiosity regarding the new fashions that no amount of persuasion or cajolery could prevent her from skating sedately into the middle of the highway in order to get a closer look at what was passing. She was not interested in the less expensive vehicles; she recognized style and saluted speed. Figures, she seemed to say, were not what they were; this new line was too low for real elegance. The old grace, the old dignity, where were they? The old politeness, where was it? That impertinent little red piece roaring by had almost touched her. Had it supposed that she would move aside to give it passage? No, indeed. And this extraordinary-looking little bicycle making such a hideous noise—she really must have a closer look at that.

'I'm all to pieces,' said Joss, and wiped the sweat of fear from his brow. 'You take over and see what you can do. The damn steering wheel doesn't seem to have any connection with the car at all.'

Sebastian took the wheel and the car continued to go its own way. When a sports car travelling at over a hundred miles an hour bore down on them and the big black car missed it by inches, the Comtesse leaned forward to bang on the glass partition separating her from the drivers.

'What are you doing?' she shouted angrily. 'Please pay attention! Can't you drive properly? Why do we stay all the time in the middle of the road? We—There! Be careful, I tell you.'

Sebastian, fighting grimly to control the car, made no reply. Joss, beside him, was making some calculations.

'It's about seventy kilometres—roughly forty miles—to Rennes,' he said presently. 'We've driven, if you call it driving, for exactly an hour, and we've done under thirty.'

'Miles?'

'Kilometres.'

'What's the time?'

'A devil of a long time past lunchtime. I'm

hungry.'

'So'm I. What was the place the Comtesse picked out as a lunch stop?'

'Tinteniac. We'll make it just about in time for dinner.'

'Well, I'm not going to starve for anybody,' said Sebastian. 'We shall stop at the next likely-looking village we come to, and we shall all pile out and eat. Did you hear what she said about paying?'

Everybody had heard. The Comtesse had slid open the partition to announce that they would all pause, briefly, to lunch at Tinteniac; she would pay for her own lunch and for that of the two drivers, but she would not pay for the drivers' wine. For the other, the small boy, the pest, the devil who had throughout the journey refused to sit, who had danced continually upon her corns, who had chattered without ceasing of his grandfather and his aunt; for him, who had come in the car uninvited, unwanted, she would certainly not pay. Was she not giving him free transport to his home? Nobody would expect her to do more. Nobody, certainly, would expect her to empty her pockets by feasting him on the way.

'She works,' said Joss thoughtfully, 'on the system of save-the-sous.'

This was true. The Comtesse, who had shown no hesitation in buying a taxi, displayed considerable resistance to the disbursement of small sums. The glass partition had saved them

58

most but not all of the calculations she had been making regarding the expenses of the journey. When she was not adding up, she was upbraiding the unmoved Maurice. Her moods alternated between good nature and irritation, but in both, her devastating frankness did not desert her.

'Tell you what.' Sebastian spoke out of a long silence. 'We'll—'

The plan was never outlined. The car had given a sigh and a jolt and was now lurching, with none of its former dignity, all over the road.

'What is the matter?' called the Comtesse. 'Has the steering mechanism become broken?'

'No.' Sebastian, with difficulty, brought the car to a stop at the side of the road. 'Puncture, I think.'

They got out and inspected the wheels; one of the back tires was flat.

'What is it?' asked the Comtesse, stepping down in the wake of Maurice. 'Can it be blown up again?'

'We'll have to change the wheel, if there's a spare,' said Sebastian.

There was a spare wheel, but there was not, at first glance, a set of tools; it was Maurice who discovered that the cushions of the back seat concealed a jack and some rusty wrenches. Joss and Sebastian removed their coats and set to work; Maurice took off his jersey and gave some useful aid; the Comtesse walked up and down impatiently.

'What is this?' she asked at last. 'Can't you change a tire, two strong men like you? My chauffeur, I can tell you, would have done it in half the time.'

'The jack,' Sebastian told her, 'doesn't work. In fact, it isn't a jack at all; it's something made to look like one. The more you try to jack up the car, the deeper you drive the jack into the tarmac. Those holes you see in the road were made by us.'

'Then we must stop somebody who is passing,' said the Comtesse, 'and ask them for some better tools. Little boy, go into the road and wave your arms.'

Maurice, standing in the middle of the road, waved his arms with a will. Cars drove past him, almost over him; drivers performed prodigies of skill in missing him by inches; but nobody stopped.

'This is a shocking thing,' said the Comtesse at last, red-faced with anger. 'This is a matter for the police, I think, that people do not stop to give aid. Why should all these cars go by and care nothing? I shall risk myself to stop them.'

She stepped into the road, took up a firm stance in the middle and stood stock-still, her arms stretched out stiffly to the sides. Her attitude and her attire gave her an appearance not unlike a scarecrow's, but almost at once, whether from alarm or from curiosity was not clear, two cars stopped simultaneously. From one emerged two stout Frenchmen in black berets; from the other a fair young man of Scandinavian appearance. The Comtesse, no doubt encouraged by her success, stood unmoving as a Ford, two Citroens and a Cadillac drew up, their occupants disembarking and announcing their willingness to be of assistance. An unidentifiable yellow car had drawn up; a Daimler was slowing down. Sebastian signalled it on, stepped into the road and took the Comtesse firmly by the arm.

'That's enough, Comtesse,' he said. 'We've got enough reinforcements. Sit down on the grass over there and relax. We'll sort out the guests.'

He turned to find everybody talking at once. The two Frenchmen in berets, after a brief inspection of the black car, said that it was interesting, but only to antiquarians, and drove away. The two young Frenchmen in the Citroen offered tools, searched their car for them, failed to find them, laughed heartily, apologized and bowed their farewells. The sole occupant of the yellow car, a powerful-looking Frenchman, told them that he came from the nearby village and offered to tow the black car to its garage. The Englishman in the Ford said that he was terribly sorry, chaps, but he was a bit behind schedule and ought to be pushing on. The party of Americans in the Cadillac took two photographs of the black car and one of the Comtesse at a distance calculated to include the elastic-sided boots and then said that as there seemed to be plenty of guys on the job, maybe they'd better beat it. Sebastian, measuring those remaining for strength and skill, retained only the Norwegian youth and the big Frenchman in the yellow car; with these to render intelligent aid, the attempt to jack up the car was resumed. But when the damaged tire was off the ground, no tools could succeed in removing the wheel. Rust had taken a death-grip which could not be loosened. The men laboured, sweated and swore, and finally eased their aching muscles and admitted defeat. The Comtesse heard them and broke in with an impatient question.

'I do not understand; why can the wheel not be changed? My chauffeur by himself alone—'

'Yes, yes, madame.' The big Frenchman undertook to explain. 'But see, it is not possible. I will show you.'

While he showed her, Sebastian's attention went to Maurice who, standing at the roadside, was removing his shirt and shorts.

'Hey, you're exposed to the public view,' he said. 'What d'you think you're doing?'

'I'm hot, and there's a river.' Maurice pointed. 'I'm going in to get cool.'

He walked up a shady little lane, and Joss and Sebastian, mesmerized by the picture of coolness and relaxation, stood for some moments gazing longingly at the stream.

'Looks good,' commented Sebastian. 'I wouldn't mind cooling down. Look, why can't we have lunch here?'

'Off what?' asked Joss.

'Where there's a village,' said Sebastian, leading Joss rapidly towards it, 'there are shops. Where there are shops, there are provisions. You get the food and I'll get the fruit and the wine.'

Laden with packages, they walked back along the hot road and saw the Comtesse beckoning impatiently.

'Where have you been?' she called. 'This is not the time for shopping. I am waiting to go on. That car—' she gestured towards the black—'is useless. It will be taken away and we shall go in the yellow car. Please change all the luggage.'

'There isn't room in the yellow car,' pointed out Sebastian, 'for the four of us and our luggage and that Frenchman. We—'

'He is not coming,' said the Comtesse.

'He owns the car, doesn't he?' asked Sebastian.

'He does not own the car. I own the car. I have bought it,' announced the Comtesse. 'And now please pay attention and have all the luggage put from one into the other. Where is the little boy? Call him and tell him that we are going.'

'We're not going, Comtesse.' Sebastian's voice was inflexible. 'We're lunching here.'

'Here ... on the road?' asked the Comtesse in a high voice.

'There, bcside a cool stream in a shady lane,' said Sebastian. 'If you've bought the car, we'll swap the luggage, but we're not moving until we've eaten.'

He gave her no opportunity to argue. While Maurice busied himself with the change-over of the luggage, Sebastian initiated the Frenchman into some of the mysteries of the black car's engine; the transaction had been one of part-exchange, and the new owner showed no dissatisfaction over his share of the bargain. Joss helped to push it to the garage, and when he returned, he saw that Sebastian had backed the yellow car into the lane and spread rugs on the ground for the Comtesse's comfort. Maurice was splashing in the stream; the two men spread the food on to a rug and the Comtesse's expression changed gradually to one of keen anticipation. There were long, crisp loaves and fresh butter; there was cheese, of both mild and strong kinds; there was a ten-inch length of red sausage smelling alluringly of garlic. There was sliced ham and there were peaches, a melon and two large bottles of wine.

The two men washed their hands, pulled Maurice out of the stream and sat down to eat, and at once it became clear, especially to Maurice, that if anybody wanted to keep up with the Comtesse, he would have to eat fast.

He put up a good performance, but he was handicapped by the fact that the Comtesse had a longer reach as well as a larger capacity.

When the meal was over, a feeling of lassitude crept over the adult members of the gathering. Maurice's energy was undiminished; unaware of medical opinion on the subject of bathing immediately after meals, he ran down the bank and plunged into the water. Sebastian lay on his back, one arm shading his eyes. Joss propped himself against a tree and, fascinated by the Comtesse's uninhibited behaviour, allowed his curiosity to overcome his better feelings and watched her out of the corner of his eye. She brushed the crumbs from her lap, loosened the belt of her dress, tensed her muscles and gave vent to a series of low, wheezing belches. Her hands fumbled at her waist, jerking to loosen her corsets. Something irritated her thigh and she scratched vigorously through her skirt. Bending forward, she undid the middle button of both boots; after this, she leaned against a tree, folded her hands on her stomach and closed her eyes. Her hat slipped sideways, her mouth fell open, her snores rose whistlingly. Joss turned to survey her and his eyes roamed in wonder down her unclean and untidy person and rested at last on the boots stuck stiffly out in front of her.

'They remind me,' he said in a low voice to Sebastian, 'of those old blood-and-thunders.'

'What remind you?' came sleepily from Sebastian.

'Those boots.'

'Why?'

'Because they were the kind the heroine always wore. And when she was wearing them, she always walked across the railway track. At least, she walked halfway across and then she couldn't go any further.'

'Found she was on the wrong line?'

'No. Her boot was stuck.'

'And then the express arrived?'

'No. The hero arrived first. And the heroine screeched, "Save me. Save me—"' the Comtesse stirred and Joss lowered his voice cautiously—'and then—'

'What's she screeching for?' enquired Sebastian. 'Because her boot's stuck?'

'She's just heard a whistle in the distance.'

'The hero?'

'The express. And up comes the hero.'

'Up where from?'

'Well, along comes the hero and—'

'—pulls the boot out.'

'He can't. It was stuck fast.'

'So he pulls fast, but not fast enough, and the express runs over them both. To be continued.'

'He pulls and pulls,' went on Joss doggedly, 'but his frenzied attempts to free her footwear are unsuccessful and so he whips out his knife and—'

'—hacks off her leg.'

66

Joss gave up. Leaving his heroine on the line with the hero sawing madly at her boot, he closed his eyes and felt peace stealing over him. The morning's tumult and confusion flowed out of his mind. Events fell into place; they were no longer stranded travellers swept up to assist an eccentric comtesse; they were holiday-makers, newly arrived in France, seated on cool green grass, full of good French food and wine. The sun was warm—

He was roused disagreeably by the voice of the Comtesse, and opened his eyes as she woke, rose and sounded the reveille all in one movement.

'Come, why do we not go?' she called. 'We are still here, wasting time, and I am in a hurry. A picnic is good; it is a rest and that is why I suggested to have one, but we cannot stay here all day. Little boy, come out of the river at once. You—' she approached Sebastian and stood looking down at him, and for one tense moment Joss thought that she was going to prod him with her foot—'wake up, wake up, pay attention. Come along. The picnic, why is it not disposed of?'

Sebastian opened his eyes and lay looking up at her with loathing. Unwillingly, they prepared to leave. Maurice dressed himself slowly. Joss strolled into the woods and the Comtesse, a stranger to delicacy, shouted to him to be as quick as possible.

They got into the car; Joss backed it slowly

on to the main road; Sebastian craned his neck to guide him out of the lane. When they were on the road, he addressed Joss in a cautious and puzzled undertone.

'I say, Joss.'

'Well?'

'Did you happen to see that car go by just now? Just when we were backing out of the lane, I mean.'

'No,' said Joss. 'Why?'

'Because ... well, it's a funny thing, but it looked to me to be the one we saw at St Malo. The one Jessica de Vrais was going to Paris in.'

'Why couldn't it have been the same one?'

'Because in the first place,' said Sebastian, 'this isn't the way to Paris, and—'

'They could have changed their minds,' suggested Joss.

'They could. But wherever they were going,' said Sebastian, 'I got the idea, just now, that they weren't going together.'

Joss thought this over.

'You mean,' he said at last, 'she wasn't in the car with him?'

'No, I don't. I mean,' said Sebastian, 'that he wasn't in the car with her.'

CHAPTER FOUR

Their progress after lunch was slow, but it was steady. In one respect, at least, the yellow car was a great improvement on the black: it answered to the helm. Its cruising speed, however, was only thirty miles an hour, and attempts to get anything more out of the engine resulted in prolonged and ear-splitting protests. The Comtesse refused to agree to Sebastian's suggestion of stopping in order to make some adjustments and improvements; it was going, wasn't it, she asked; then let it go. Her chauffeur could have been trusted to know what to do, but she was not prepared to take the word of strangers as to their mechanical ability. She had hoped to be at home long before this, and people had gone out of their way to place obstacles in her way; let her now be allowed only to press on as swiftly as possible.

Her remarks, now that there was no partition to screen the drivers, penetrated to their ears with disagreeable clarity, but soon they turned off the main road and began twisting through narrow lanes, and her voice became a rumbling undercurrent to their leisurely progress. Only half-listening, Joss and Sebastian settled down to a drowsy appreciation of the scenes through which they

69

were passing. The countryside became greener, more wooded; the afternoon grew warmer. The Comtesse, recognizing familiar landmarks, thought of her home and grew reminiscent.

'I am not expected,' she said, 'but what does that matter? It is good to come and go without warning; if people know that you are coming, they prepare; they hide away whatever they wish to and show you only what they will. It is better to come suddenly; you find out what is being wasted, what is being thrown away. Last time, I came at night, and how many lamps were burning? Five. How many lamps are needed for one person? One, isn't it so? If you are in one room, you do not need to keep the lamp in another.'

'Lamp?' repeated Joss curiously.

'Lamp, yes. Do you think that I would agree to having electricity? Do you know what that would cost for a chateau? It would cost a fortune, and for what? Why should I have electricity? I am not there so much; shall I have electricity to be wasted all the time I am away? No, I am not so stupid. That is the thing about me that everybody learns: that I am not stupid. When people think that I am, they find out that they are mistaken. That is why I have come back from England so quickly and why I came at so much expense and with so much hurry—to show somebody that I am not to be treated like a fool, like an idiot. Oh, but I shall show him!'

Sebastian half-turned to look at her curiously.

'Someone done you down?' he asked.

'Done—Yes, that is what they have done. It is not good English, but it is the truth. I have been cheated. I have been robbed.'

'Did somebody break into the chateau?' asked Joss.

'To steal? No, nobody did that. If they did, I would have called that honest cheating. A thief who comes to your house says to you, "I will try to take your things; if I am caught, all right, I will go to prison." But a thief who thinks he takes no risk, now that is dirty cheating. When somebody of your own family takes from you and says, "I am quite safe; she will not ask the police to come because I am her kinsman"— that, too, is dirty cheating. But I am not, as I told you, a fool. Let us only get to the chateau and I shall find out whether what I suspect is true. That I have been cheated, this I know already; but there is one—I mention no name—who imagines that he has a right to the chateau. In my absence, who shall say that he has not established himself, taken possession, made himself, as the English say, at home? Soon, I shall find out. Can this car not go faster? We have been on the road for—'

'Look,' yelled Maurice.

The shout made Joss jump from his seat. For most of the journey, Maurice had been leaning

71

against his shoulder and breathing down his neck, but he was totally unprepared for the yell.

'Do that once again,' he said threateningly, 'and you'll walk the rest of the way.'

'Look!' repeated Maurice, unheeding. 'Cloisy!'

They looked at the village coming into view, and as they came nearer, they saw that Cloisy was indeed Lysaine, and Lysaine, Cloisy. The two villages were separated only by an old stone bridge which, spanning the narrow river, began in Cloisy and ended in Lysaine. Lysaine, which they could see beyond the bridge, looked little more than a hamlet, but as they drove towards Cloisy, Joss saw to his joy that it was everything he expected of a French village. There was an épicerie with rows of tight black or red sausages hanging above the counter; there was a boulangerie with loaves several feet in length, a clinical-looking charcuterie and a small but picturesque roadside café with tin tables set out on the pavement under a striped awning. There was a primitive water pump, there were little boys in dark pinafores. The whole was something Joss had hoped for but not expected to see: a tiny, typical, unspoiled corner of France.

Across the bridge, at Lysaine, things looked very different. There were two or three dispirited-looking shops, some shabby houses and that was all. But the background was one of great beauty. Fields bordered the road, but beyond the fields were thickly wooded slopes which almost encircled the two villages.

They were not to cross the bridge. Before it was reached, Maurice pointed to a narrow lane that branched to the left just near the village of Cloisy.

'Down there,' he said.

'This is Cloisy; that, over the bridge, is Lysaine,' the Comtesse told them.

'Why don't they signpost it?' asked Sebastian. 'The signpost we passed only mentioned Salvan.'

'Salvan is more important. But those who live at Cloisy or Lysaine,' said the Comtesse, 'know where these places are; they do not need signposts to tell them. And nobody else wishes to know. Why should they? What is there to bring strangers here? These are small villages, no more; the people who live in them do not wish to attract howling mobs. And at Lysaine, the land is nearly all mine and I do not wish to have signposts leading people to it.'

Sebastian was turning into the narrow lane. Maurice had lowered one of the windows and was hanging half in, half out of the car. The weariness of travel was suddenly dissipated; excitement mounted. Maurice was in familiar surroundings and was thumping Sebastian excitedly on the back.

'There is it! Our house!' he shouted.

He pronounced it houth; after much patient

pulling, he had succeeded in extracting a second tooth; he fished in his mouth, rescued the tooth, dried it tenderly and wrapped it in his bloody handkerchief.

'You can't go inside the gate,' he told Sebastian, stuffing the handkerchief into his pocket. 'You have to stop outside.'

Sebastian slowed down; to the right was a small wooden gate; he brought the car to a stop beside it.

'This is very nice,' he said slowly.

The gate opened on to a large garden. Down the centre of this ran a flagged path leading to the front door of the house. It was not a garden to delight horticulturists, for there were no flower beds, but its grass was green and close-cropped and shaded by magnificent trees, and it looked a place in which small boys could amuse themselves without doing damage; if the garden proved too confining, there were fields adjoining it on one side and orchards on the other. In one corner was a small lily pond, in another a small summerhouse. Beneath one of the trees was a long wooden table with benches, giving a pleasant suggestion of meals eaten out of doors.

The house was painted a pale shade of pink; its name, *Marielle*, was on the wall in small black letters. It was a long, low, rambling house, and it was the only one in view on this side of the lane; on the other side, three or four chimneys could be seen showing through the

74

trees.

'This is where your grandfather lives?' the Comtesse asked Maurice in surprise.

'Yes. And Tante Francine.'

'Then you are the grandson of Monsieur d'Arnaud?'

'Yes.' Maurice grappled with the car door, pushed it impatiently and shot out into the lane. He picked himself up, grinning, opened the gate and ran along the path and up to the front door. He banged impatiently on its panels, chanting as he did so.

'Grandpère! Tante Francine! Céline! Tante Francine!'

There was no response. Joss and Sebastian, standing at the gate, saw that the house was shuttered and its doors closed; nobody came to answer Maurice's summons. It became clear at last, even to him, that nobody was at home. He turned.

'Where are they?' he demanded indignantly. 'Nobody comes.'

He spoke in French; his precipitate descent from the car seemed to have shaken out of him all traces of his Jersey strain; even his gestures had become French.

'They've probably gone to meet you,' said Sebastian. 'It's what we more or less expected.'

'What is going on?' enquired the Comtesse from the car.

'They're not here,' said Joss.

'So much is clear.' She got out of the car and

75

came to the gate. 'When will they come? How shall we find them? Am I to be delayed because they wish to be out when they should be in?'

'They're probably stuck somewhere between here and St Malo,' said Joss.

Sebastian walked up the path.

'If your grandfather couldn't get to St Malo, he would have let somebody here know, wouldn't he?' he asked Maurice. 'Wouldn't he have telephoned to somebody to leave a message for you in case you rang up? There's no telephone in the house. Where would he—?'

'He would telephone for Céline,' said Maurice.

'Telephone to Céline, you mean.'

'No, not to; for. He would telephone to Madame Seyboule to tell Céline.'

'Who is this Céline?' asked the Comtesse.

'She is the servant who comes every day to work, to clean the house,' said Maurice. 'Her house is close to Madame Seyboule's.'

'And which is Madame Seyboule's?' asked Sebastian.

'There.' Maurice pointed to a red roof to be seen through the trees on the other side of the lane. 'Shall I go and see her?'

'No, no, no,' said the Comtesse. 'Go and find the servant, this Céline, and let us have the house opened and you and your luggage disposed. Go on, go on.'

Maurice sped through the gate, across the lane and vanished in the woods beyond. The two men walked slowly round the house, looking at it from every side.

'Nice place,' commented Joss.

A wide, flagged terrace ran along the front of the house, level with the grass; three or four doors opened on to it. There was no garden at the back; there was only a wide courtyard and, in the distance, the woods.

They walked to the gate and found the Comtesse growing irritable.

'Why should we wait?' she asked. 'We have come here, we have brought the boy to his relations and it is not our fault if they are not here to receive him. If they went to meet him, they should have left somebody behind to receive him in case he came. If there is a servant, she will take care of him. I wish to—'

She stopped. A yell had come from Maurice; he was running back, and behind him came a stout, middle-aged peasant woman. Maurice, arriving breathless, jerked his head in her direction.

'She comes—Céline,' he said. 'Tante Francine telephoned this morning. She was at the station and she said that there were no trains and so she and Grandpère were driving back as fast as possible.'

'Driving?' repeated the Comtesse. 'Driving?'

'If they were driving,' asked Sebastian, 'why couldn't they have driven to St Malo?'

'They are not in a car. There is no car,' explained Maurice. 'Grandpère would like to have one, but Tante Francine says no, because there is not enough money. She—'

'Yes, yes, yes; we have heard all about this Tante Francine,' said the Comtesse. 'If they are not in a car, what are they in?'

'The waggon,' said Maurice. 'They go in the waggon to the junction at Salvan, and leave it there in the stable and take the train.'

'But ... but look here,' said Joss. 'If they telephoned this morning, they must have been on the point of coming back here. It's now after five; they couldn't possibly have taken all that time.'

'Here is the woman; she will explain,' said the Comtesse.

Céline had arrived at the gate, but excitement and haste and the pleasure of seeing Maurice had combined to rob her of the power to speak. She stood before them, panting, apologetic, drawing in deep breaths and pointing to her heart to indicate that this was not the sort of thing that did it any good.

'Now really!' protested the Comtesse. 'How long must we wait? If she cannot speak, can she not open the house?'

'She has no keys,' said Maurice. 'Tante Francine took them away because she did not know that there would be any delay. Céline told me.'

'Oh, this Tante Francine, Tante Francine,' moaned the Comtesse. 'All the day, in my ears, Tante Francine. It is too much.'

'Madame—' Céline had recovered her breath.

'Good,' said the Comtesse. 'Now we shall hear.'

Before Céline could utter one more word, there was a cry from the lane. They turned to see a small, thin, grey-haired, wiry-looking woman running towards them. She arrived as breathless as Céline had done, but unlike Céline, she did not wait until her normal breathing was restored before saying what she had come to say. Coming to a halt before them, she drew in a long, deep breath that came through her pinched and indrawn nostrils with so shrill a whistle that the Comtesse moved back a pace and stumbled against the gate.

The whistle was the signal for the flood waters to open. Immediately after it, Madame Seyboule announced herself and launched into a stream, a torrent, a cascade of words. She had much to say, and she said it with no pause save for the whistling breaths she drew when she ran out of air. They were here, she told them, in the expectation of giving the little Maurice to his relations? Only this morning Tante Francine had telephoned; there were no trains and they had set out at once to return from Salvan. But (whistle) there had been an accident, a small accident, nothing to make anxiety, but still an accident. Maurice could witness how she had always warned that the waggon was not safe (whistle) in these days when automobiles went *phtt* this way and *schtt* that way without regard to safety, and now this was proved, for upon leaving Salvan, a car had passed (whistle) and at the moment of passing, had made a devil's noise upon the horn, upon which the horse had without hesitation entered a side road and the waggon, as one can imagine (whistle) could not turn as easily as the horse and it had sunk with two wheels into a ditch and although Our Lady had watched over Monsieur d'Arnaud, preserving him from harm, he had (whistle) received a shock. But in the car following, there had been a doctor, which is proof of the goodness of God, and the doctor took monsieur at once into his own house, which was near (whistle) and said that he would not allow him to continue his journey until he had rested for one night with him. Tante Francine wished, naturally, to stay with him and so she had asked if she, Madame Seyboule (whistle), would explain this to anybody who should telephone from St Malo to find out why Maurice had nobody to meet him. She, Madame Seyboule, had promised to do this, and also to keep the boy safe (whistle) with her for the night when he arrived, but since that moment, what had unfortunately occurred? the water in her house had ceased to flow, making who knows what inconvenience and what danger to health and (whistle) thus for her it was impossible to admit anybody, and it was with joy, with relief that she had observed

80

that the Comtesse, who lived so near and in so large a chateau, had undertaken to bring the boy to his home and who would now find no trouble in driving on to the chateau with him and (whistle) keeping him for this night only, and in the morning he would be claimed by his own, who would bless the name of the Comtesse, and she, Madame Seyboule, could rest with an easy mind and take her leave with lightened heart (whistle) and say au revoir, Madame la Comtesse; all revoir, messieurs; Maurice, all revoir.

The last farewells came from the gate, the lane and the woods; the last whistle seemed to the outraged Comtesse one of triumph. She was, however, too exhausted to speak. Throughout Madame Seyboule's monologue she had protested, shouted, stamped her feet—to no avail; the speech had gone on to the end.

'But ... how is this?' she croaked hoarsely at last. 'I am to be saddled with the boy?'

Sebastian looked round for Maurice, but he had vanished.

'I suppose so,' he said.

'But these people—I do not know them. I do not receive them. I did not know, when I brought the boy, that he would be the grandson of this d'Arnaud. I do not like the family at all. Why should I allow that whistling creature to push the child without invitation into my home? Why should I take him?'

81

'He can sleep under my bed,' offered Sebastian. 'I don't really see that anything can be done about it. You can make your protests to Tante Francine in the morning. After all, it's only for one night. Shall we go?'

'Yes,' said the Comtesse gloomily. 'Where is the boy?'

A startled exclamation from Céline told them where he was. He was on the roof, hanging precariously over the edge.

'Hey, come down!' called Sebastian.

'By this way,' shouted Maurice, 'I can get into my bedroom. I know how to get in. I have got in before.'

'Let him,' said Joss.

They watched him in silence. Maurice swung himself down, secured a foothold, bent to reach the window of the room just below him and the next moment had pushed it open and was scrambling inside.

'Wish I had a shilling for every time I'd done that,' said Joss. 'I wonder if Tante Francine ever caught him at it?'

Maurice came down and opened the front door and then ran back through the hall and out of sight. Céline followed him, and after some hesitation, Joss and Sebastian went in and found her in the kitchen, buttering a crust of bread for Maurice.

'You'd better bring that with you,' advised Joss. 'You've kept the Comtesse waiting long enough.'

'I would ask her to come inside—' Maurice spoke in muffled tones through a large mouthful of bread—'but she will not come. Céline told me just now. She's a Catholic and we're not and so she doesn't like us. We're Protestants.'

But Protestants or not, curiosity, or a stranger attraction, had drawn the Comtesse into the house. When Joss and Sebastian had brushed the crumbs off Maurice and led him into the hall, they saw to their surprise that she was coming out of the drawing room. Something in her manner made the two men look at her suspiciously.

'Where is ... there he is, the little boy,' she said, her tone so sugary that Maurice stared at her in surprise.

'I'm ready to go,' he told her.

'Ready? Yes, yes, of course.' The Comtesse was doing her best to inject a tender note into her voice. 'We are all ready; soon we shall go to the chateau, which you will like very much, very much indeed. All boys,' she informed him with a wide and ingratiating smile, 'like my chateau very much. Very much indeed. I make them happy there. I give them bonbons and I let them play just how they like, and I allow them to go into the gardens and climb the trees.'

Maurice, his head on one side, was regarding her with a mixture of interest and suspicion.

'And then?' he enquired.

'Then ... oh, you shall enjoy yourself, I promise you. You shall see when you are there. And now tell me something, little Maurice—it is Maurice, is it not?'

'Maurice Pierre—'

'Yes, yes, yes. Well, Maurice, come in here.' The Comtesse turned and walked into the drawing room and the others followed her. 'You see this little table? Your grandfather does not want it in here, surely? It is very ugly. I am sure that he would like to sell it.'

'But Tante Francine—'

'Ah, I know what you would say! There are many things that your grandfather wants, and Tante Francine cannot give them to him, is it not so? So this is what I am going to do: I am going to take away the ugly little table that nobody likes and I am going to leave some money for Tante Francine. She will be very pleased, you will see. She will have money to buy your grandfather the things that he wants.'

'An automobile?'

'Ah, you joke! You are having a little joke! But I will get the money.'

She opened her bulging black bag and thrust her hand inside. Groping, she produced a roll of franc notes, put them on the table and groped for more.

'See,' she told Maurice, snapping the bag shut and holding up the money. 'I will put this into this vase here and tomorrow you shall hear how pleased your aunt will be. And I will take away this ugly little table.'

'No, you won't,' said Sebastian quietly.

She swung round on him belligerently.

'Why should you interfere with my affair?' she demanded.

'I'm not interfering in your business; I'm not even interested,' said Sebastian. 'But you can't—'

'You wish to say that I must come here tomorrow with a more formal proposal to buy the table? Tomorrow I shall be in Paris. Do you not understand that these people will be happy to sell the table? I have not paid less than its value, and you will believe me when I tell you that there is not a woman in France, in Europe, who knows better than I the value of furniture. Am I running away with the table? No. I have left a good price. In the morning, these people will come to take the boy; if then they have any objection to make, let them return the money and take back the table. It is informal, but I am in a hurry. But without the table, I do not go. I do not leave the house. You are a stranger here, but I have lived here for many years; shall I not know better than you what they would like?'

Sebastian had nothing to say to this. He raised his eyes and met Joss's glance. Argument, Joss seemed to be saying, is useless; let's get out of here and explain the matter to these people in the morning.

He stood aside. The Comtesse picked up the table and handed it to Joss.

'Come, let us go. It is only four kilometres to the chateau. Bring the boy; what is one more thrust upon me? Bring Napoleon's army; come.'

They went out to the car and Sebastian handed the Comtesse into it; Joss backed the car out of the lane. Céline stood waving, and as they turned into the road, a handkerchief fluttered from one of the windows of Madame Seyboule's house.

They were going in the direction of the bridge, but for a brief instant, Sebastian looked back at the road which led to Salvan. Then he was staring at Joss, his expression one of stupefaction.

'What's the matter?' asked Joss.

'That car again,' said Sebastian. 'I'll swear it was there again.'

'Hallucinations,' diagnosed Joss. 'What would it be doing anywhere near here?'

'It was going in the direction of Salvan. But why? And why is she alone? What's happened to this fiancé fellow?'

'I think you're just seeing a car of the same kind and colour,' said Joss. 'You told me they were going to Paris, to get married. Would a man, or a girl, back down at that stage? And even if they did, why would anybody want a back-of-beyond place like Salvan? What's more, it was his car and not hers, so she'd hardly be circling the country in it all by herself, would she?'

'I suppose not. All the same, I'm pretty sure that it was the green car and that Jessica de Vrais was driving it. I haven't the least idea why, but ... it's a funny thing...'

'Well?'

'I've got a feeling,' said Sebastian slowly, 'that we're soon going to find out.'

CHAPTER FIVE

The four kilometres between Lysaine and the chateau had a picturesqueness that only Maurice did not appreciate, since he had curled himself up on the seat beside the Comtesse immediately on leaving Cloisy, and was now fast asleep. Joss drove into the thick woodland that engulfed the road immediately the bridge was crossed, and then the trees had given way on one side to the high wall bordering the grounds of the chateau.

'Here my land begins,' said the Comtesse. 'It is pretty, I think.'

'It's beautiful ... and unspoiled,' said Joss.

'Certainly unspoiled. Who shall spoil it?' asked the Comtesse. 'If tourists come, there is no hotel, no inn here or at Cloisy. The road does not go on after the chateau and so they must turn and go back again.' She leaned forward and pointed. 'There, on the left, the gate.'

They turned into a wide gateway and drove for some distance along a winding drive. The drive straightened out into a tree-lined avenue, at the end of which was a forecourt. Beyond this, huge and grey and spreading, stood a beautiful eighteenth-century chateau.

Joss and Sebastian looked at it with an admiration in which there was a good deal of surprise. They had not been certain of what they had expected to see, but nothing about the Comtesse, except the aristocratic nose, had given promise of anything as genuinely imposing as this. Whatever the state of the building—and there were signs of neglect everywhere—nothing could detract from its cold, calm beauty.

'You like it?' asked the Comtesse.

'Like it?' echoed Joss. 'It's ... it's beautiful.'

'Yes, it is beautiful,' she agreed, and there was a shrug in her voice. 'But it has ruined the family who owned it for so long. I am glad that I have no son to talk to me of the pride of the de Chandillots. Where there is debt, how do you speak of pride? I have heard too much of all this and that about tradition and symbols and upholding dignity. For all the years of our marriage, my husband said nothing else. Some men throw away their fortunes on horses, on women, on wine or gaming, but what ruined the men of this family? This chateau. Now what is left? The money is gone and the last Comte de Chandillot also, and now this

88

chateau, what is it? It is a storehouse, a warehouse, a place where I keep the furniture that I buy and sell.' She leaned forward and pointed. 'Stop there, at the little door. We do not now use the central entrance.'

They stopped before a low, ivy-hidden doorway. Before anybody could assist her, the Comtesse had hurried out of the car and was pulling impatiently at the cord of a bell above the door. She pulled often and impatiently, muttering angrily as she waited. At last there was the sound of slow footsteps and the door was opened by a tall, thin old man. The Comtesse addressed him in rapid French.

'I am back, as you see, Léon. I came back in a great hurry. Tell me with truthfulness— Monsieur has been here?'

Léon had given a stiff little bow, but showed no sign of emotion; he answered his mistress calmly. Nobody, he said, nobody at all had come to the chateau.

'You are sure that nobody could have got inside without your knowing?'

Léon was quite certain.

'Then I am not too late,' said the Comtesse. 'When he comes, I shall be ready for him.' She gestured towards the car. 'Bring the luggage in.'

Joss and Sebastian helped to unload the luggage, leaving Maurice undisturbed. Without a word, the Comtesse led them down a narrow stone corridor and through a door at the end. Joss and Sebastian followed her and then halted and looked round them in amazement.

They were in a vast stone hall about forty feet high. It was, with the exception of two or three suits of armour, completely bare. A beautiful staircase curved up to a high gallery; here hung some tapestries, but there was no sign of any furniture. The early evening light, streaming in through the high windows, gave the scene a theatrical, almost a dramatic appearance. The stark cold struck through the visitors' clothing, and Sebastian gave a shiver.

'Yes, it is cold,' said the Comtesse. 'Come, I shall show you where you are to sleep.'

They followed her across acres of marble floor, through another door, along another corridor and up a flight of stairs. They crossed a wide landing and began to climb a second flight, less grand, more steep. This ended in a long gallery, and along it the Comtesse led them, pausing impatiently now and then to wait for them as they lingered behind.

'You look for furniture, perhaps?' she said. 'There is plenty of furniture, but I do not keep it out in the rooms. I keep it only where I need it. There is only Léon to work here; he cannot look after half, a quarter of this place, you understand? So the furniture is stored, shut away. I will show it to you tomorrow.'

They were on their way up yet another staircase; the Comtesse began to pant and her steps became slower. The stairs ended on a narrow landing, and a chill, this time an inward one, fell upon Joss and Sebastian; they had obviously come to a part of the chateau to which guests of consequence were not shown. The walls were damp, the rooms on either side small and mean.

But there was still another flight of steps to be climbed, this time of stone, narrow and winding; they were in one of the circular towers. The Comtesse's breathing became so laboured that Joss went past her and gave her a hand to pull her up; even this was not enough, so Sebastian put his hands on her hips and levered her up from below.

'There! We have arrived at last,' she panted.

They were on a small landing. To right and left were doors; the Comtesse, opening them, disclosed three bedrooms, all small, all mean, all cheerless, with a few items of furniture that looked fit only for firewood.

'Now you will be comfortable,' she said.

'I don't think we'll be comfortable at all,' said Sebastian coldly. 'These, I imagine, are servants' rooms?'

'Certainly they were at one time servants' rooms,' admitted the Comtesse readily. 'But these are the only rooms with beds, don't you see? Tomorrow, if you wish, you shall choose other rooms and I will give you furniture, but you will have to move it yourselves, and this evening it is too late. I will send Léon to you

91

with sheets; you must make the beds yourselves, because he will be attending to other things, you understand?'

The men did not reply; they had scarcely heard her last remarks. They had glanced out of the windows of one of the rooms, and the view had rooted them to the spot; enchanted, they were looking out over the spread of countryside below, far below. They were at the top of one of the towers, high above the trees, and Lysaine and Cloisy were toy villages hidden in a sea of green.

'It is a good view, of course,' said the Comtesse. 'From so high, you can see much.'

Sebastian turned to her.

'What time is dinner, Comtesse?' he asked.

She stared at him with some displeasure.

'Dinner? You expect dinner?' she asked in surprise.

'We expect to eat,' said Sebastian.

'Eat, certainly; but when you say dinner, that means that you expect something to be set before you, and who shall set it?'

'How about Léon?' suggested Sebastian.

'Léon? He is attending to me. Perhaps in half an hour, if you go downstairs to the kitchen, he will make you some omelettes, but you must not expect, when I live here alone, that I shall keep food for an army. I said to you at St Malo that you shall stay here if you wish, but I did not promise to provide banquets. You must go to the kitchen and speak with Léon and

92

arrange something with him. You must eat there; I do not use the dining rooms. I do not use any rooms; only one, which I keep for myself.'

'I don't quite understand,' said Sebastian. 'Do you mean that the entire chateau is unfurnished?'

'Certainly. I have said so more than once, but I think you do not listen properly. The furniture is all gathered together in certain rooms; I keep only enough for my own use. I have my meals taken to my room. And now I shall leave you because I have important telephone calls. We shall meet, perhaps, in the morning, when the boy's relations come to take him away.'

She left them, and Sebastian stared at Joss with a black frown of anger.

'If I'd known this—' he began.

'It's a bed for the night,' pointed out Joss calmly. 'I don't suppose the mattresses will be too damp; these rooms must get pretty warm in summer.'

'I wish we'd dropped the old hag and driven on to a decent hotel.'

'She's an interesting character,' said Joss thoughtfully.

'She's an eccentric and rather unpleasant old woman who goes to any lengths to provide herself with what she wants and doesn't give a damn who or whom she uses on the side. What I can't understand is why there was all this

93

howling hurry to get back to this place.'

'She's on somebody's tail, I think. The idea was to get here before whoever it is who's been doing the dirty cheating. I'd like to see all that furniture she's got stored away.'

'I'd like to see some thick steaks and some potatoes and—What's that noise?'

The noise was caused by Maurice, who had come up the narrow staircase dragging a suitcase.

'You're awake, are you?' said Joss, as he came into the room.

'Yes. I went into the kitchen and saw Léon and he said to bring this case because it isn't the Comtesse's.'

'Well, it isn't ours either,' said Sebastian.

'Good Lord!' Joss was staring at it. 'It's—'

Sebastian looked from his face to the suitcase.

'It's the big brother,' he said slowly, 'of the set—' He stopped and gave a long, low whistle. 'So that's why she's driving round the country! She's looking for us.'

'But you said that she went in the direction of—'

'—of Salvan. So she did. So would we have done if the Comtesse hadn't been with us to show us where Lysaine was. If Jessica de Vrais is trying to find this place, she'll have a hard time of it. But where, as I said before, is her fiancé?'

'I don't know. But I'm sorry about the case,'

said Joss.

'You needn't be,' said Sebastian. 'It's my fault for not looking to see that Maurice loaded the luggage properly at St Malo. You asked me, and I meant to do it, but I was busy gazing at that black car's inside. I ought to have known that a boy who wrote his name on other people's luggage would naturally begin to feel he owned it. I should have watched him.'

Maurice had dragged the suitcase to the bed and was lifting it on to the mattress. 'Whose is it?' he asked.

'It belongs to a girl who came over on the boat from Jersey,' Sebastian told him. 'And if she's really driving round looking for it,' he added to Joss, 'instead of going to Paris and seeing about getting married, then there must be something in it that she wants pretty badly.'

'How would she know we had it?' asked Joss.

'That's easy. There was a good proportion of the local population watching us as we left St Malo; somebody'd be sure to remember a princely piece of luggage like that one. She'd ask who saw it, and where, and they'd produce the bleary-eyed taxi driver and he'd tell her where we'd gone. The only thing I can't understand is why that fiancé isn't with her. You'd think he'd want to—'

'*Tiens!*'

The exclamation came from Maurice in a squeak of surprise. The men swung round and

95

then stood staring. He had been experimenting with the clasps and they had opened; he had lifted the lid. They were looking at the white folds of the wedding dress.

'Well!' Sebastian spoke softly at last. 'Now we know why she's looking for us.'

Joss walked forward and put a finger gently on the circlet of orange blossom.

'Wonder if this'll delay the wedding?' he mused. 'But—' he turned to Sebastian—'if she found that we had the case, and if she came to find us, why didn't she get here ahead of us?'

'First,' said Sebastian, 'because, like all women, she's probably incapable of reading a map. Even if she read it correctly, she'd have a hard time finding her way through all those lanes we came through. Another likely theory is that she took off in a flaming temper—she must inherit it from Papa—and she hasn't cooled down enough to be able to find the right road. But she'll get here. She's got as far as Salvan; they'll send her back here, and it had better be soon if she wants to get to Paris tonight with the bridal raiment. She'll—Look, Maurice, will you stop playing about with that suitcase and shut it up and leave it alone?'

'I was only seeing if it had got a tray, that's all,' said Maurice. 'But it hasn't.'

'Well, stop handling property that doesn't belong to you, and—My holy aunt!' ended Sebastian, slowly and reverently.

There was a long silence. Joss and Sebastian,

staring, found nothing to say. They were looking down, fascinated, at the bright and gleaming objects to be seen among the folds of the wedding dress.

'Aren't they pretty?' said Maurice. 'They shine.'

Sebastian, with a strong effort, pulled himself together.

'Go downstairs, Maurice,' he ordered, 'and look round and see if you can find a decent bathroom we can use. The one we've been given is two floors down and has *c* but no *h*. Find one with both hot and cold water, and then come back and report to me.'

Maurice slid off the bed and ran happily down the stairs.

The men stood staring down at the gleaming jewels disturbed by Maurice, jewels hidden deep in the folds of the dress, secured by thread from the danger of slipping out of place. Only Maurice's rough handling had disturbed them.

'Do you see those, Joss?' asked Sebastian slowly.

Joss had seated himself on the bed and was bending over the case to look more closely.

'Jewels,' said Sebastian. 'In the dress— jewels. And,' he added with conviction, 'worth a packet.'

Joss looked up.

'B-but ... but that's s-smuggling!' he stammered.

'And in a big way.'

'But ... if she's caught! I mean, if she'd been caught. If they'd—'

'If they'd done a bit of rummaging? What Frenchman would put a finger in there after seeing the wedding dress and getting a mental picture of the bride—that bride—wearing it? A Frenchman is a Frenchman first and a Customs official next; he probably fell into a sentimental reverie and chalked up the score without a second glance.'

'But why risk—?'

'Wedding presents,' guessed Sebastian. 'Her wedding gift from Papa, I don't doubt. They look to me like heirlooms. The idea of getting them through the Customs inside the wedding dress was probably all his own.'

'No.' Joss spoke positively. 'No, it couldn't have been his idea, because everything I heard in Jersey said that he was against the marriage. In fact, I'm fairly certain that nobody— certainly not her father—knew that she was coming over to marry this fellow.'

'You mean that she came without her father's consent?'

'His consent wouldn't make much odds; she's over twenty-one. I think she came without his knowledge.'

'Are you trying to say that she brought the loot without his knowledge, too?'

'I'm trying to believe that she didn't.'

'Well, it's going to be interesting to meet her again,' said Sebastian, closing the case after rearranging its contents carefully. 'It was going to be pleasant anyway, but now it's going to be even more so. Here comes that prying, sneaking son of Satan, with no idea of how grateful I am to him. Well, Maurice?'

'The bathrooms,' reported Maurice, 'don't have hot water. Only cold water. All except two, right downstairs on the ground floor. One is the Comtesse's.'

'Then the other,' decided Sebastian, 'will be ours. It'll take a week to get to it, and two weeks to get back up all those stairs, but it'll be worth it. And now let's see about getting some food. Maurice, you seem to have found your way to the kitchen, so you can lead us there.'

It was a long walk. When they reached it, they found a vast, dim chamber with a long row of disused ovens, a primitive heating cupboard, an antique iron spit and a wooden table some ten or twelve feet in length. In a far corner, Léon was stirring something in a saucepan on a Primus stove. He looked up as they entered and shook his head regretfully.

'There is no food, messieurs,' he told them. 'I keep enough for the Comtesse, for she comes and goes without warning, but for two, three—'

'Will it be in order for us to make our own arrangements?' asked Joss.

'Certainly, monsieur. I regret that it should be necessary, but I am here alone, you understand? I am caretaker, I am cook, I am cleaner.'

'But the chauffeur? There's a chauffeur, isn't there?' asked Sebastian.

'The chauffeur, that is also myself, monsieur. But for years there has been no car.'

'How about getting this stove alight?' asked Joss. 'Is there fuel?'

'There is wood, monsieur; I will bring some.'

'Good. I'll light the stove,' said Joss. 'Sebastian, if you'll take the car and go and buy some food, I'll cook it. If you go at once, I'll have a fire going by the time you get back; that'll give us bath water and something to cook on.'

'Come on,' urged Maurice. 'Let's go quickly.'

When the two got back, Joss was ready for them and the kitchen looked a good deal more cheerful. Cooking utensils were assembled at one end of the table and a checked cloth had been laid at the other. Joss, in his shirt sleeves, and wearing an apron borrowed from Léon, was looking with satisfaction at the glowing fire in the stove.

'Here.' Sebastian and Maurice dropped their purchases on the table. 'Bread, butter, eggs, veal chops, salad, cheese, coffee, sugar, milk, potatoes—if you're thinking of asking me to peel them, I vote we have them in their jackets—olive oil—Maurice's idea, and a good one—vinegar, lemons, salt and I think that's all.'

'That's fine. Leave me to deal with it,' said Joss. 'You take Maurice and see that he has a bath.'

'Have a bath?' said Maurice.

'Supervise his bath?' said Sebastian.

There was violent protest in both voices. Joss ignored it.

'I'll have a meal ready for you when you get back,' he said.

'But look here—' began Sebastian.

'Unless,' said Joss, 'you'd rather peel the potatoes.'

When Sebastian and Maurice returned, the latter in pyjamas and a dressing gown, the scene had become almost one of domestic comfort. Plates and knives and forks were laid ready; Joss was bending over the stove; Léon was bringing in more wood; there was an appetizing smell.

They sat down to eat; Léon, following a code of his own, insisted on removing his plate from the cloth to the bare board and then sat down happily to the meal. The chops were juicy and tender; there were fried potatoes and potatoes boiled and mashed with butter; there was crisp salad with a breath of garlic; the bread was scrunchy and the butter rich and golden.

They were eating heartily, silently, when the door opened to admit the Comtesse. The men rose and she advanced into the room sniffing the air appreciatively.

'I knew that you were eating something

101

good,' she told them. 'I passed by the door, and the smell came out to me. Perhaps there is something left for me? Léon does not give me enough; a small omelette, and he thinks that is a feast. This is veal; that is good, I like veal.' She sat down and looked expectantly at Joss. 'As a rule I do not eat meat at this time, but after a journey one is hungry, isn't it so?'

She was given a plate, a knife and fork and some food. Léon, still following his code, took his plate and slipped quietly away. The Comtesse ate quickly and with the silent concentration she had shown at lunch; the meal over, she pushed away her empty plate, loosened her skirt band and looked at Sebastian.

'In the morning, it may be that I must go to Paris,' she told him. 'I do not know for certain; I am waiting for a telephone call. If I have to go, you will drive me?'

'All we contracted to do, Comtesse,' Sebastian told her, 'was to drive you to Lysaine. After that, you said, we would be free to go or to stay; there was nothing said about driving you anywhere else.'

'But don't you understand that it is simply for the reason that the trains are not going? Would I ask you to drive me if the trains were not striking?'

'Yes, I think you would,' said Sebastian. 'Is there any reason why Léon shouldn't take you to Paris?'

'Léon? But Léon has to work in this place. Shall I go away and leave the chateau full of strangers? That would be extraordinary, I think. We have the car, and you are doing nothing. But see,' she went on before either of the men could answer her. 'The little boy has gone half to sleep. Call Léon. Léon, take the child upstairs and put him to bed. Now pay attention,' she resumed, as Léon led away the glassy-eyed Maurice. 'I will explain something to you about why it is necessary for me to go to Paris. I will begin at the beginning.'

'One moment.' Joss held up a hand and rose from the table. 'Coffee.'

He walked to the stove and brought the coffee to the table, but the Comtesse had risen.

'Bring it to my room,' she said. 'It will be better to talk there.'

They followed her along a corridor, through a circular hall, through several empty rooms and into another hall. From this opened a long, narrow, pleasant room which overlooked the drive by which they had approached the chateau. Here, at least, there was no lack of furniture; the room was full of showpieces. At one end were tables, chairs, sofas of every period; at the other, uncurtained, was the huge four-poster in which the Comtesse slept; beyond it were three or four beautiful dressing tables.

'Put the tray there.' The Comtesse pointed to a small table exquisitely inlaid with mother-of-pearl. 'Sit down, and we shall make ourselves comfortable.'

Joss put down the tray and drew up a chair for the Comtesse; she poured out the coffee and handed it round and Joss took his cup and looked at her expectantly.

'You were going to say something?' he reminded her.

'Yes. This is what it is. I have a nephew,' she told them. 'I could tell you many things about him, but I will say only that he is a no-good. I have tried to help him, but it has all been useless. For years I kept him here; I paid for his education, but I saw that he would never be of any account and so at last I threw him out. I sent him away. I gave him money every year and let him go on his own way. For many years I have not let him come to the chateau, and I do not like to see him because I do not like him. But last week I found myself in a difficulty, just as you were this morning at St Malo before I came to help you. This difficulty was, I had to be in two places at the same time. There was a sale in Paris, and a sale in London. I—'

'Sale of what?' enquired Sebastian.

'Of what?' she echoed irritably. 'Of furniture, naturally. Do I sell cows and sheep? Well, this is what I am explaining. Both sales were very important to me, and I wished to be at both, but naturally I could not, but I found out that my nephew was in Paris and I decided that I would ask him to go to the sale there and

104

buy for me. And so I asked him. I did not want to; I did not trust him, but also, I did not trust anybody else. He agreed to buy, and then I made this mistake: I gavc him the money. It was a great deal of money; the furniture in which I am interested is not cheap. I went to London, and there I waited after the sale for him to telephone to me and tell me how much he had paid for the thing that I wanted. But no word. No sign. And at once I made enquiries and I found that no, he had not been to the sale at all. So where is my nephew? Where is my money?'

'Well, where?' asked Sebastian after a pause.

'That is what I am waiting to hear now. I did not think that he would ever cheat me, openly like this, with defiance. I thought that he would be too frightened. But when I understood that he had taken so large a sum of money, my money, I said to myself that he would not stop at that. Having taken so much, he would take more. I was sure that, knowing me to be in London, he would come down to the chateau and help himself to some of my furniture. He knows good furniture; so much, at least, I was able to teach him. And that is why I wished to come here without delay, and at whatever cost; I was willing to spend much because I wished to catch him here. As you see, he has not yet come, but I am sure that he will. I have telephoned to make enquiries and I am waiting to hear if there is news of him. All that I know at present is what he told me himself.'

'And what was that?' asked Sebastian, as she paused.

'There is a woman,' said the Comtesse.

'That's no surprise, is it?' asked Sebastian.

'In a way, yes. In a way it is a surprise. Like all the men of his family, he spends freely, but he does not spend on women. So it is a surprise, now, to learn that he is in the hands of a woman. He said that he was going to marry her, and that she was very rich. I did not believe him, and now you can see that he was lying. If a man is to marry a rich woman, he does not need to steal from his aunt; he can steal from his wife. But if this woman thinks that she is going to enjoy my money, she will have a great surprise. I—'

She broke off abruptly. The telephone beside her bed had begun to ring shrilly. She went eagerly across the room to answer it.

'Now,' she said, 'I shall know what he has done; perhaps even where he is.' She lifted the receiver and bellowed into it. 'Allo? Allo? I am here. Speak.'

There was a pause, broken only by the muffled sounds coming through the telephone. Joss and Sebastian, watching with undisguised interest, saw on the listener's face blank astonishment, indignation and finally outrage.

'Impossible!' she exclaimed at last. 'He would not dare! You are quite certain? Yes ... yes. Then he has gone to see this woman, you say? In the car? Yes ... yes, I am listening. Green, you say?'

The others were only half-listening. Attracted by another sound, they had turned to look out of one of the great windows and were following with absorbed interest the progress of a car which had come up the drive and was circling into the forecourt. It was in full view of the Comtesse, but her attention was on the details coming over the wire.

'You do not know the number? But green, a sports car with a ... a—what is that? Yes, yes, a green dragon on the front and ... yes ... I am ...'

Her voice died away. She had raised her eyes and gazed, at first absently and then with eyes and mouth opening in stupefaction at the car which had come to a halt almost in front of the window. Her hand seemed to become lifeless; without heeding the sounds still coming from the telephone, she fumbled the receiver back on to its stand and stood staring out at the car standing on the drive in the gathering dusk. Her voice, when at last she could speak, sounded dazed.

'But ... that is it,' she said slowly. 'That is the car. That is the same one, and if it is the car, it must be also the woman.' She turned to stare at the others. 'But then where,' she enquired, 'is my nephew?'

Sebastian was already at the door.

'Let's go and find out,' he suggested.

CHAPTER SIX

It was some time before the visitor was admitted; the chateau, as Joss and Sebastian had already learned, was not a compact building. They had some distance to cover; while they covered it, Jessica stood at the great front door and tugged repeatedly at a bell which Joss thought must once have hung in the belfry of a cathedral. As the booming sounded again and again, the Comtesse, hurrying to keep up with the men's long strides, panted her uncomplimentary opinions of the newcomer.

They reached the main hall and Sebastian struggled with bolts; soon the door swung open. Jessica stood before them—but for some moments, nobody seemed able to find anything to say.

The Comtesse, perhaps, experienced the greatest surprise. She had fashioned in her own mind, when listening to the voice on the telephone, a full-scale model of the kind of woman with whom her nephew would be associating. To adjust her sights to this slender, haughty young woman standing on the steps took time. Sebastian was hesitating because he had seen beneath Jessica's coolness signs that things were not as well with her as they had been when he had addressed her on the quay that morning. She looked pale and tired and there was a good deal less confidence in her bearing. But if she had lost her confidence, her temper, he saw, had not gone with it. Before the Comtesse could speak, she had addressed her in French in a low but biting tone.

'I shall be glad to know, madame,' she said, 'why you took away from St Malo this morning a suitcase which did not belong to you.'

The words shook the Comtesse out of her newly recovered poise.

'Suitcase?' she echoed blankly.

'We have it,' Sebastian told her calmly. 'Perhaps this young lady may enter?'

He had spoken in French, a fact which always appeared to infuriate the Comtesse.

'My English, as you know,' she grated, 'is as good as yours. Come in, mademoiselle,' she added to Jessica, 'and do not begin to ask questions of me; there are things that I shall ask of you first.'

She turned and led the way to her room and the others followed. Sebastian fell into step beside Jessica and looked down at her curiously.

'You look tired,' he said. 'Lose your way?'

'You,' pointed out Jessica coldly, 'had somebody to show you where Cloisy was. It isn't marked on any map and it isn't shown on any signpost and nobody has ever heard of this Cloisy. I was sent miles in the wrong direction, and went round in circles until somebody suggested that I might want the Cloisy near Salvan.'

'We saw you twice. Didn't you see us?'

'I was looking for a black car. You left St Malo in a black car. What's that yellow one out there?'

'We did that to confuse you.'

'Where's my suitcase?'

'Upstairs. Right at the top of one of the towers. It's safe, and so,' he added expressionlessly, 'is everything in it.'

Her glance went to his face, probing, but before she could speak, they had reached the Comtesse's room.

'Now,' said the Comtesse, 'we shall sit down and then—'

'There's some coffee left,' broke in Joss quietly, 'but it's probably cold by now.'

'I'll have it, hot or cold,' said Jessica.

Joss brought the cup to her and the Comtesse looked at her searchingly.

'Please to tell me who you are,' she requested.

'I was your nephew's fiancée,' said Jessica. 'He can now consider himself released from the engagement. At least, I suppose he's worked it out by now. I didn't stop for the formalities.'

'You found out, I suppose,' said the Comtesse, 'that he did not mean to marry you?'

'I found out that he had bought the car with your money,' said Jessica. 'That was enough to go on with. I hope you get your money back on it, but I'd like to have the use of it to get me to an hotel tonight.'

'You're not going anywhere tonight,' said Sebastian. 'I am sure that the Comtesse wouldn't hear of it. Have you eaten anything since lunch?'

'No.' Her voice was resigned. 'I got hungrier and hungrier, but I couldn't believe it would take me so long to find this place, and so I didn't stop to eat.'

'There are some veal chops left,' said Joss. 'Could you eat them?'

Jessica rose.

'Show me,' she begged.

'Come.' The Comtesse assumed the role of hostess. 'We shall go to the kitchen and you shall eat there because it is warm and comfortable. There are chops, and perhaps we shall find some salad and potatoes and some cheese and some fruit. I did not expect you and so you cannot complain of my hospitality.'

'I'm not complaining.' Jessica stood at the door of the kitchen and gave a wondering look at the vast and dimly lit spaces.

'Sit down. I shall sit here,' said the Comtesse, 'and you will eat and talk to us. I wish to know everything.'

'Then you must ask your nephew,' said Jessica, who had sat down, shaken back her hair and was watching Joss and Sebastian eagerly as they prepared food for her.

'But where is my nephew?'

111

'The last time I saw him, he was a few yards away from the Customs shed at St Malo, going north,' said Jessica. 'He came to meet me this morning; he arrived with a car and we were going to drive to Paris, but one of my suitcases was missing. We found that you'd taken it, but when he heard your name, he—'

'Ah! I can see all,' said the Comtesse. 'Naturally, he would not come himself for the suitcase and so he sent you, the coward.'

'He didn't send me. I came.'

'You left him there?'

'Yes.'

'You drove away in the car?'

'Yes.'

'Good. That is good,' said the Comtesse. 'Now he has no car and no fiancée. I suppose,' she added casually, 'you are rich?'

'I'm not; my father's said to be.' Jessica smiled up at Joss as he placed two cold chops before her. 'Thank you, this is wonderful. Yes, heaps of potatoes, please; yes, lots of salad.'

'He was going to marry you for your money?' pursued the Comtesse.

'Or for her beauty,' pointed out Joss gently, 'or her exquisite figure, or her lovely skin, or—'

'Yes, yes, yes,' agreed the Comtesse. 'All those things, naturally. But without money, he could not afford them. All his life he has wanted money.'

'Then you should have seen that he was equipped to earn some,' said Jessica, between

112

mouthfuls. 'He's not stupid; he could have been trained to do something.'

'For years,' said the Comtesse angrily, 'I have given him money.'

'And that's where you made a mistake,' said Jessica. 'What he needed was a job.'

'You think, my clever mademoiselle, that he would have worked?'

'Not in a routine job, perhaps. Not in an office.' Jessica selected a crisp leaf of lettuce and crunched it with enjoyment. 'Not as a nine-to-fiver. But he could have helped you, he said, to buy and sell furniture. Only you wouldn't let him.'

'You speak of things you do not know about,' said the Comtesse coldly. 'And also, mademoiselle,' she added shrewdly, 'you speak very calmly of a young man who only this morning was your fiancé. There was not much love, perhaps, in this contract?'

The colour rose in Jessica's cheeks and the Comtesse, content to have scored a point, rose to her feet.

'I am going to leave you,' she said. 'It is I, now, who will have some news to say on the telephone. When you have finished your meal, mademoiselle, these gentlemen will show you a room in which you may sleep tonight. Tomorrow you will please get your own breakfast; my servant, Léon, will be too busy to attend to so many. It is getting dark, but no lamps are prepared for you and so you must use candles; you will find them in the little box near the stove.'

Sebastian opened the door for her, closed it behind her and walked back to the table. He sat with Joss opposite Jessica, and for some time they watched in silence as she ate. Presently she gave a long sigh.

'I feel alive again,' she told them.

'Then you've got to thank us and not the Comtesse,' said Sebastian. 'We bought the food and we cooked it.'

'I cooked it,' corrected Joss. 'The Comtesse's idea of hospitality embraces bed and board yourself. It's not a bad idea; I'm going to use it next time Sebastian comes to stay with me.'

'It serves us right,' said Sebastian, 'for allowing ourselves to be picked up by strange comtesses.'

'Why did you come?' asked Jessica.

'She was in such a hurry to get back to the chateau that she bought no less than two cars to do the journey in. She offered us the job of driving them, and as there seemed nothing better on hand, we came along. We heard the story of the no-good nephew; she was certain, I think, that he'd taken over the chateau in her absence.'

'If he'd had any sense, or any courage, he would have done,' said Jessica. 'It's odd, isn't it, that the two of them didn't come face to face on the quay.'

'It's a great pity,' said Sebastian regretfully.

114

'It would have been a scene worth watching. Or listening to.'

'Are you sorry you came here?' asked Jessica.

'No,' said Sebastian.

'No,' said Joss. 'The Comtesse isn't exactly attractive, but the chateau's interesting and the village is pretty—at least, Cloisy's pretty, not Lysaine. On the whole, I think I'd like to stay on here, as the Comtesse suggested.'

'So would I,' said Sebastian, 'but not in those rooms in the tower. There's a lot of furniture stored away; I don't see why we shouldn't install ourselves in a couple of decent rooms and borrow enough stuff to furnish them and make ourselves comfortable for a couple of weeks. We can keep ourselves and we can pay for our accommodation by driving the Comtesse here and there on reasonable journeys in the neighbourhood. She invited us here; she won't lift a finger to make us comfortable, but I think I can persuade her to let us fix things up as we want them. What,' he asked Jessica, 'do you intend to do?'

She looked down at the tablecloth, her fingers absently following the line of the checks. Sebastian rose, got glasses, poured out wine and carried it to the table.

'Why don't you stay here, too?' Joss asked Jessica in his slow voice.

There was no reply from Jessica; she was still tracing patterns on the tablecloth.

'I don't want to sound interfering,' Joss went on with some hesitation, 'but I did gather, from the rumours going round in Jersey, that your father—' He paused. 'Did you tell him that you were coming over to be married?'

Still no reply. Jessica's finger still moved along the lines, but presently a tear appeared on her cheek and rolled slowly down and was followed by another; soon twin streams were coursing down and she was fumbling angrily in her bag for a handkerchief.

'Here,' said Sebastian.

She took his, shook it open and dabbed her face.

'I'm . . . It's just that I'm tired,' she muttered. 'I—'

'Go ahead and cry,' advised Joss gently. 'It'll do you good.'

'No, it w-wont,' sobbed Jessica. 'It doesn't do me any g-good and I'm a f-fool. I h-hate crying. I never cry. It's just that I—'

'Don't talk; have a good howl, as Joss advised,' said Sebastian. 'He does it frequently.'

Jessica gave a short, tremulous laugh and dried her eyes firmly.

'I'm just being an idiot,' she said.

'No, you're not,' said Sebastian.

She took out a small mirror, looked into it and gave a moan of horror.

'I look t-terrible!'

'No, you don't,' said Joss. 'You look very

116

nice.'

'We like you far better like this,' pointed out Sebastian, 'than we do when you're being overbearing.'

'Over—'

'—bearing,' he repeated. 'You look, at this moment, very nice and womanly. If women don't cry every now and then, they become dried-up, and they crackle, like the Comtesse. Drink your wine. When you've finished it, we'll take you up and show you your room, which is far from ritzy but which has a magnificent view which you'll be able to see in the morning. You shall have the biggest room and I'll have the next biggest and Joss'll have to go in with Maurice because it serves him right for looking the kind of man trusting mothers load their children on to.'

'Who loaded him?' asked Jessica.

'His mother, on the quay at St Helier this morning,' said Joss. 'His grandfather and his aunt didn't turn up to collect him, and we found they lived at Cloisy, so we brought him along and they're coming to fetch him tomorrow.'

Sebastian raised his glass.

'Well, here we all are,' he said, 'and perhaps it'll be fun. I drink to the de Chandillots.'

'Hubert, too?' asked Joss.

'Hubert most of all, poor devil,' said Sebastian feelingly. He rose. 'Come on,' he said to Jessica. 'Bed. Where are those candles?'

Only two candles could be found; by the light of these, they made their way through the ghostly, echoing rooms to the great hall and out into the drive to bring in Jessica's luggage. Then they found their way, by a system of trial and error, to the rooms in the tower, and found that Jessica, like the Comtesse, needed assistance up the last flights of stairs.

'Here we are,' said Sebastian, as they reached the top. 'Quiet, or we'll have young Maurice up and about again.'

Jessica stood looking round her room in the flickering candlelight.

'You needn't say anything,' said Joss. 'Sebastian and I said it all.'

'It's only for tonight,' said Joss. 'Oh—' he went out and returned with the missing suitcase—'here you are.'

'Thank you,' said Jessica.

Joss put it on a chair and his eyes met those of Sebastian. Don't say any more, he signalled, and Sebastian nodded. They went out quietly and closed the door behind them, and Jessica, left alone with a solitary candle, walked slowly to the window and stood looking out into the darkness. Tears of exhaustion, of regret began to pour down her cheeks, and she let them fall. They were right, those two; it was good to cry. It eased the heart . . . a little. But tears could not wash away mistakes. Tears could not blot out all the years of stupidity which had led up to this supreme act of folly. Shame filled her and made her cheeks burn. Her father, she understood now, though a difficult old man, had had a difficult task. If he had been irritable, she had given him cause. And she had set out from Jersey that morning with only one end in view, however she might have disguised it. She had had only one desire: to prove to her father, conclusively, that she could be trusted to know her own mind, that she was capable of making reasoned and sensible decisions and that she was as able as he himself was to assess a young man's character and intentions. She had liked Hubert, and she had persuaded herself that she loved him. He had deceived her, but she had wronged him by using him as a weapon to defeat her father. Her determination to get the better of her father had led both Hubert and herself into this trouble, for if she had not encouraged Hubert in the summer, he would in all probability have gone away without asking her to marry him; if she had not agreed to marry him, he would not have stolen his aunt's money—for stealing it was. She would not have...

She closed her eyes, and a sob escaped her. She was proud; she had held her head high and it was not easy to face the humiliating truth. But if Hubert had stolen, so had she. Hubert had used his aunt's money to buy a car in order to impress her. She had taken her mother's jewels to ensure that in the event of Hubert's being what her father had declared him to be, she would not have to return home in ignominy. The jewels were to be hers, but she had taken them from her father's safe and she had cheated her way past the Customs. Lies, and deceit. They were harsh truths, but she had to face them. She had lied and cheated because she had been cursed with a temper—her father's temper—and had never troubled to control it. It flared hotly in her father, but it was balanced by his sound sense, his shrewdness, his knowledge of the world; in her it had raged without check. She had intelligence, but her temper had swamped it; she had ideals, but her temper had swept them away. She was here in an echoing French chateau, surrounded by strangers, tired and defeated and humiliated, because she had allowed her temper to take control.

She turned, sobbing, and undressed and groped her way to bed. Still weeping quietly, she fell asleep.

CHAPTER SEVEN

In the morning, the green car was no longer outside the chateau; Joss and Sebastian, preparing breakfast in the now warm and homely kitchen, speculated on what had become of it.

Léon, coming in with a tray on which was

120

the remains of the Comtesse's breakfast, explained its disappearance. The Comtesse, on the previous night, had ordered him to drive it into one of the garages; indicating two huge keys hanging from a hook behind the door, he added that the door was doubly padlocked. The Comtesse, who entered the room as he was speaking, added a further comment.

'Without the keys, nobody can get in and nobody can get the car out,' she said. 'Did you think that I would leave it outside all the night, for anybody to come and drive it away? I am not so stupid. Good morning. I hope that you slept well.'

Joss and Sebastian, returning her greeting, said that they had slept intermittently.

'Bats,' explained Sebastian, holding out a warm plate on to which Joss carefully shovelled a golden omelette. 'If you have a moment, Comtesse, I'd be glad to know—'

'—what I wish to do? I will tell you.' The Comtesse sat down at the table, looked round for Léon, found that he had vanished, and asked Joss to bring her an extra cup. Sebastian, after looking pointedly into the coffeepot as if measuring its contents, poured out some coffee for her. 'I will tell you,' she said, helping herself liberally to hot milk. 'I made a bargain with you, and I always keep my bargains. I said that if you came here, you could stay if you wished. This also suits me very well, for I have some business to do very often, and if there are no

121

trains, then of course I must go by some other way, and as I have bought a car, why should you not drive me?'

'I told you, Comtesse,' said Sebastian. 'We don't mind taking you on reasonable trips, but not—'

'The journey to Paris, that I am not taking. It was on account of my nephew, and now there is no need. But soon there will be other sales, and I do not see why you should not take me. In return, you may make arrangements for yourselves here to be more comfortable.'

'How much more comfortable?' enquired Sebastian. 'We need—'

'Ah, so you make terms?'

'A bargain,' said Sebastian, 'is usually a two-sided affair. You've stated what you want, and now I'm stating what we want: rooms on the ground floor, since there doesn't appear to be a bathroom with both hot and cold water on any of the other levels; some furniture from wherever it's stored, and—'

'It is valuable furniture, you understand?'

'We'll use it carefully and do it no harm. We shall buy our own food and fuel and attend to all our own needs; at the end of two weeks we shall replace the furniture and leave the place as we found it.'

'Well, all right.' The Comtesse drained her cup and pushed it forward for more coffee; Joss, with a convincing air of not having noticed the gesture, poured the contents of the

122

pot into his own and Sebastian's cups. 'Very well, you shall—Why is there no more coffee for me?'

'I thought you had had your breakfast,' said Joss. 'We saw your tray come out.'

'Léon does not make good coffee. Well, never mind. I agree to this that you have asked, but remember that I do not wish to be disturbed; you must choose rooms far from mine.'

'But yes,' murmured Sebastian into his coffee.

'And this girl, when will she go?' the Comtesse enquired.

'I don't know. She isn't up yet and we came down without disturbing her,' said Sebastian. 'But we hope that she'll stay.'

'Stay here?' asked the Comtesse in astonishment.

'Why not?' asked Sebastian in turn. 'Your nephew has behaved very badly and—'

'Fft, fft, fft.' The Comtesse waved an impatient hand. 'She is not a child, and nobody but a child, a stupid child, could be deceived for one moment by Hubert. What he is, is plain for everybody to read; he is good-looking, for all the men of his family are good-looking, but it is the good looks of an unformed boy; nobody could place upon him any trust, any reliance. He is not to be taken for one moment seriously. If she loved him, she got it all over very quickly. Which is more, if she was to be married to him,

123

where are her parents, her family, her friends? Were they not to have been present at the marriage? And are they not at this moment enquiring for her? I am not a fool; all this seems very strange to me. She—'

'She eloped,' said Joss mildly.

'She—' The Comtesse stared at him with her mouth open. 'She made to elope with Hubert?' she said wonderingly after a time. 'With Hubert? It is not possible that she should be so—so—'

'Her father,' said Joss, 'is a man well-known in Jersey. He—'

'Jersey? The island of Jersey?'

'Yes. He is well-known and much respected,' went on Joss in his deliberate way, 'but he has rather a bad temper and—'

'Ah!' The Comtesse wagged her head. 'You need not tell me any more. He threw Hubert across La Manche and this stupid girl followed. And do you think that I shall keep her here, against her father's knowledge, against her father's—'

'We shall send him a telegram this morning,' said Sebastian, 'telling him that the wedding's off and she's staying here with you. He'll probably give you all the credit for having saved her from your nephew. And we shall look after her and take her away with us when we leave the Chateau.'

'And how,' demanded the Comtesse, 'shall I assure myself that nothing will take place under my roof that—'

Her words faltered and withered under the long, hard look of open dislike which Sebastian was directing at her.

'You were saying, Comtesse?' he asked coldly.

'I was saying something very sensible,' she said, 'but if you are going to look so surprised about it, then I must pretend, I suppose, that you two are not very well-looking men and that the girl is totally without attraction. This is the modern way, and what it leads to, we all know. Which is more, between men and women there is only one way to make a rule: no opportunity, no sin. This I believe, and this all parents should act upon. But you are nothing to me and so I shall wash my hands.'

Joss and Sebastian, glancing involuntarily at the grimy members she was using to emphasize her words, felt that washing would greatly improve their appearance. Joss saw that she was wearing the garments in which she had travelled—and dined—the day before; he was willing to believe that she had slept in them. He tried for a moment to imagine her life in this great, bare chateau, with only Léon to wait upon her, with nobody of her own kind to see or to speak to, with no amenities and few comforts, but found it too difficult. Then he heard her addressing him.

'Where is the little boy?' she asked.

'I don't know,' said Joss. 'He wasn't in his

bed when I got up, and he wasn't in the room.'

'He came down early and he had some breakfast with Léon,' the Comtesse said. 'Then he went outside, but where, I do not know, and it is not good to let him go anywhere where he cannot be seen. I hope that he is not doing any harm. If his Tante whatever-her-name-is does not come soon, somebody must take him to his home.'

She went out, and a few moments later the door opened again and Jessica made a cautious entry.

'She gone?' she enquired.

'Yes. Come on in. How did you sleep?' enquired Sebastian.

'Beautifully, thank you.'

They looked at her. The contrast between her fresh, groomed appearance and the frowsiness of the Comtesse was so striking that they found themselves smiling at her in frank appreciation.

'What's the matter?' she asked. 'Do I look odd or something?'

'You look like the morning,' said Sebastian. 'Sit down and I'll get you some breakfast. Eggs, some of yesterday's potatoes fried up, a bit of—'

'Just coffee, thanks,' said Jessica.

'Oh, come!' protested Sebastian. 'I'm a good hand at breakfasts.'

There came from Joss a laugh of such pure amusement that Jessica looked at him and smiled in sympathy. He put his hands on the table and leaned on them to address her.

'He has never,' he told her slowly, 'made breakfast in his life, except occasionally in his London flat, when he's found himself temporarily without slaves. He's about as domesticated as the panther. The only reason he's bestirring himself now is because, like every worm, I have a turning point. If he says that he can cook, he lies. Please refer to me whenever he makes any statements concerning his attainments.'

'I will,' promised Jessica. 'Look, don't make fresh coffee for me. I'll finish what's in the pot.'

'There's no more. The Comtesse invited herself to coffee,' said Sebastian. 'Keep your eyes on me as I make some more and you'll see that Joss didn't do me justice.' He went to the stove and spoke over his shoulder. 'Joss told me he'd met your father.'

'You have?' Jessica turned in surprise to Joss. 'You didn't tell me.'

Joss grinned.

'It wasn't exactly a social meeting. And it wasn't an amicable one, either.'

'You mean you ... you quarrelled?'

'We disagreed. I haven't got much land in Jersey,' explained Joss. 'About half an acre, to be precise. But there's a strip of gorseland below my cottage on which nobody's allowed to build—without my permission, that is. I bought the cottage with that safety clause

127

attached to it. Nobody could build much on it, because it's too narrow, but they could put up something that would blot out my view of the sea and the lighthouse. Your father—'

'Oh! Was that *you*?' cried Jessica, the words almost drowned in laughter.

'I don't know quite what that means,' said Joss. 'Your father wanted to buy the bit of land and put up a—'

'All he wanted was a tiny, glassed-in beach house so's he could get a nice view of the sunsets.'

'So I gathered. He told me something of the kind in the early part of our interview, when he could still speak coherently.'

'He came back purple,' said Jessica. 'He called you—'

'I know what he called me. He said it all to me at the time. He offered me large sums to compensate me, but how can you compensate anybody for shutting out the beauty and light that they look on to? I waited a long time for that cottage, and the cottage without the view is like … like—'

'—the Comtesse without the chateau,' suggested Sebastian.

'Something. Well, Jessica's father came and requested; then he demanded; then he bribed, and finally he threatened. He waved a blank cheque in my face and I told him that I wanted a lot of things out of life, but his money couldn't buy any of them. Then he called me an

128

egotistical and idealistic idiot and I called him ... I forget what I called him. But it must have been something rude, because he went away and he hasn't been back since.'

'You called him a mobile cash box,' said Jessica.

'I did?' Joss sounded incredulous. 'I didn't mean to go as far as that, but he's a persistent man. I hope he didn't feel hurt?'

'No, only surprised. He was under the impression—before he met you—that money only had to shout loudly enough in order to make itself heard.'

'When you go and call on Jessica in Jersey,' said Sebastian, 'you'll have to hang round waiting until her father goes out; then you can creep in.'

'Jessica can come back to the cottage,' said Joss.

'You'd like it, Jessica,' Sebastian told her. 'It's a nice place. It's got what they call character. Joss is the character.'

He brought the coffee to the table and poured some into her cup. Sitting down, he watched her drink it and then spoke slowly.

'Joss and I,' he said, 'have something to say to you. As big brothers.'

She put down her cup and looked at them both.

'What about?' she asked.

'Little boys,' answered Sebastian circuitously, 'have enquiring minds. They like

129

to take things to pieces; they like to fiddle about with things. If you don't look out—and Joss and I weren't looking out—a small boy can open the clasps of a suitcase and show everybody what's inside.'

He paused.

'Go on,' said Jessica.

'It's a very pretty wedding dress,' said Sebastian.

'I didn't know big brothers were interested in wedding dresses,' she said.

'We weren't particularly. But did you have any idea,' he asked slowly, 'of what a serious risk you were taking with the . . . other things?'

'What other things?'

'You're quite right to wait until Sebastian's more specific,' said Joss gently, 'but the dress got shaken up a good deal and—'

'—and then we saw the contraband,' said Sebastian. 'The idea was good, but the risk—I suppose you knew?—enormous.'

'We're not worrying,' Joss told her, 'about why you brought them, or even how. What we were thinking was how, now that your marriage is off, you're going to get them back into Jersey. You're well-known there, so you can't hope to get away with it again. And you can't, or you shouldn't, go about with valuable jewels lying about in an unlocked suitcase.'

There was a long silence, during which Jessica pushed her cup forward absently and as absently drew it back when Joss had refilled it.

130

'They were my mother's,' she said slowly at last. 'She left them to me, but my father wanted to keep them until I married. They were kept in a safe in his room; I was free to go to it whenever I wanted to. I brought them with me because I ... because I felt that I needed a sort of ... second string.'

'How long had you known this Hubert?' asked Sebastian.

'About two weeks. He stayed with us in Jersey. It sounds fantastic, but I ... I rather liked him. But my father said that he was a ... a this and a that, and he'd said the same things so often, and so violently about all the men I invited to the house, that I decided he couldn't be right all the time. I didn't know much about Hubert, but I was certain that he was a good deal more reliable than my father made him out to be. I felt that I couldn't go on forever producing quite reasonable men and listening to my father calling them names. I felt that one day, I'd have to follow my own judgement. I'd have to choose one in ... in—'

'In his teeth?' suggested Sebastian.

'In defiance of his opinions. And so I chose Hubert.'

'But having chosen him, and having come across to France to marry him and spite Papa, why the jewels?' asked Sebastian.

'Because, don't you see, if Hubert turned out to be the fortune-hunting little beast my father made him out to be, I wouldn't marry him, and

I certainly wouldn't go home to look a silly little fool, and so I'd need money to keep me in France.'

Sebastian looked at Joss.

'You following this?' he asked. 'Maybe I haven't got a good head for figures—or something. She was going to marry Hubert in Paris more or less straight away, but she was going to have plenty of time to study him and check up on his motives and character. If he didn't stand up to this prolonged scrutiny, she wasn't going home; she was going to stay in France carrying round valuable jewels in an unlocked suitcase. Now you go on from there.'

'She was going to sell the jewels,' said Joss.

'Piece by piece, I suppose, like a prima donna on the rocks?'

'Yes,' said Jessica.

'Who was going to buy them—piece by piece?' enquired Sebastian.

'Jewellers—or somebody,' said Jessica unwillingly. 'I know it sounds silly now, but I was angry when I thought it all up, and when you're angry ... when I'm angry, I don't think very clearly. I knew I'd need money, and I'd spent my foreign allowance. If I'd tried to get francs from somebody, it would have meant paying for them, and that would have meant borrowing money from my father, because I'd spent my home allowance, too. So I thought of the jewels, and it seemed to solve everything. I planned to stay in France for about a year and—'

'Spend the time unloading the jewels on to soft-hearted dealers who'd give you top prices and ask no questions,' ended Sebastian. 'This girl, Joss, is a credit to her seminary for young ladies.'

'I wasn't at a seminary for young ladies,' said Jessica.

'Neither was I,' said Sebastian, 'and it's a pity, because they're said to be good schools and I bet any third former could give you and me, both of us, lessons in sensible behaviour. I ought to have taken one look at Hubert and pushed him over the edge of the dock and driven you away in the green car. You should have taken one look at Hubert and—'

'I did drive away in the green car.'

'Yes. You did that,' acknowledged Sebastian, 'and it was the only spark of intelligence you showed. But to risk bringing in those jewels, to plan—'

'Big brothers,' put in Joss quietly. Sebastian looked at him blankly, and he went on in the same calm tone. 'You said we were big brothers, remember? Not policemen. Not push-arounders. Not—'

'All right. I'm sorry,' said Sebastian. 'But someone has to make this girl see sense.'

'I've seen sense. It's all over,' said Jessica.

'Until you try to get the loot back into Jersey,' said Sebastian. 'But we'll tackle that problem when the time comes. In the meantime, let me tell you what I've been arranging with the Comtesse.'

He went on to tell her, and Joss looked across the table and thought that the other two, with the coffee between them, made a charming picture of domesticity. He felt a strong instinct to go away and leave them together.

'I think I'll go and see where Maurice has got to,' he said.

He closed the kitchen door behind him and walked through the chateau and out into the clear morning sunshine. He went along the front of the building and round to the back, but there was no sign of Maurice. He came round to the front once more with the idea of searching the woods, whose trees seemed designed for small boys to climb.

He reached the forecourt and saw in front of him a sight that halted him in his tracks. He stood still for some time; he had an avid appetite for colour, and this was a feast indeed. The background was the wide grey spread of the chateau. In the foreground stood a waggon painted a vivid scarlet, drawn by a glossy chestnut mare. In the high seat of the waggon was seated a girl dressed in blue. Her hair was honey-coloured, her cheeks pink, her eyes the same shade as her dress. The eyes were on Joss, and he made no effort to break the spell that the scene had laid upon him.

Then the girl gave a flick of the reins,

brought the waggon close to him, looked down and spoke—and at her words, Joss's head spun dizzily and he found himself struggling to marshal his ideas.

It was not easy. Besides marshalling, he had to adjust—and some of the ideas were deep-rooted. He had, for example, he told himself dazedly, always imagined that French girls were dark. They were Latins, weren't they? Or were they? Anyhow, they had to have dark hair and eyes like horse chestnuts and long dark lashes; it was tradition; everybody expected it. But this girl had spoken in French and she was as English-looking as a ... a rose. That in itself was absurd; nobody but an English girl was supposed to look like a rose. And she had said—and what a beautiful voice she had; how soft, how sweet, how—But what had she said? She had stated, quite clearly, that she had come to take her nephew home. Her nephew. If she had a nephew, then she must be an aunt. If she was an aunt, then she must be—No. It was impossible. But not impossible at all. She was an aunt, and she was without doubt Maurice's aunt. She was—great heavens!—she was Tante Francine.

Joss's mouth, which had fallen open, which had in fact been open for several moments, closed firmly. He was a fool, he informed himself. He had assumed that the aunt of a boy of six must be a middle-aged or even an elderly woman; he had linked her in his mind, as

135

Maurice had linked her in his conversation, with Grandpère. Whether thirty or forty years would have to be subtracted from Grandpère's age remained to be seen; for the moment, here was Tante Francine, and she was all of twenty-two or twenty-three years old.

A smile spread slowly over Joss's face. He looked up into the girl's eyes—and then the smile faded. There was no friendly look in her eyes; they were at this moment the blue of ice, and her lips were drawn into a soft bunch of anger.

'Er ... good morning,' said Joss lamely, and realized that Sebastian would have done far better.

'Good morning. You are, monsieur,' she enquired coldly, 'one of the two Englishmen who came to our house yesterday?'

'I ... well, yes,' said Joss. 'I am. You're Tante—I mean, you must be Francine—I mean, you're Mademoiselle Carron.'

'Carron is the name of my sister, Maurice's mother. I am Francine d'Arnaud, the aunt of Maurice, and I have come to take him away. My father—his grandfather—and I are very grateful to you and to your friend for having brought him from St Malo.' If she was grateful, she didn't sound it, thought Joss disconsolately. 'But now I wish to take him home, monsieur. I wish also—' her voice became glacial—'to take the table which you took away from the house.'

'The ... Me?' said Joss in astonishment.

'You, monsieur. Or perhaps it was your friend. One of you, we were informed, took from the drawing room a table. A small table, but a good table. A valuable table.'

'No. Yes. I mean—' Joss, in his distress, found his French deserting him. 'Do you speak English?' he enquired.

'Yes, monsieur. Will you please give the table back to me again?'

Her English, though more halting than the Comtesse's, was infinitely more pleasing to the ear. But the note of coldness was still only too apparent.

'I haven't got the table,' he explained. 'I only carried it out for the Comtesse. She ... she bought it.'

'She did not buy it,' stated Francine calmly. 'She stole it. And in carrying it out of our house, you—'

'Oh, but half a minute!' protested Joss. He moved a step nearer to the waggon and stared up at her. 'The Comtesse—I mean, I don't for a moment condone her methods, but she did pay for it.'

'The money that she left in the house is here.' Francine held up an envelope. 'She can have it back again. We do not want it. Please will you take it to her and bring the table to me?'

She held out the envelope and Joss took it and held it unhappily.

'If you'll come inside,' he suggested, 'we

can—'

'No, monsieur. I will not enter the chateau. I do not wish to speak to the Comtesse. I have not met her and I do not want to meet her. If you will take the money—'

'Tante Francine!' Maurice's delighted yell broke into the sentence. 'Tante Francine!' He raced up to the waggon and clambered into it, speaking rapidly in French. 'When did you come? Where is Grandpère? Did you fall out of the waggon yesterday? Madame Seyboule told us. Did you—?'

'I think,' said Joss to Francine, 'that you'll have to have a word with the Comtesse. Won't you—'

'I will not go into her house,' said Francine.

'Then ... then look, Maurice,' said Joss, 'will you go in and tell the Comtesse—'

He stopped. Jessica and Sebastian had come out and were standing watching the scene. A moment later there was a shout of laughter from Sebastian, and he took Jessica's hand and brought her up to the waggon.

'I'm willing to bet it's Tante Francine,' he said. 'Good-morning, Tante Francine. Do you know that we all thought you were a tartar of an old lady who lived only to put the brake on Grandpère?' He put out a hand to help her down. 'Come in,' he said.

Francine ignored the hand. Her voice was calm and cold.

'Please,' she said to Joss, 'will you explain
138

everything.'

'Well, it's like this,' began Joss unhappily. 'She—'

'I know. She wants her table back,' said Sebastian. 'Good. I like to see the Comtesse baulked.'

'But she says that we're, as it were, accessories after the fact.'

'How does she make that out?'

'I carried out the table.'

'Then you're obviously an accessory. But I,' said Sebastian, 'did nothing, nothing at all but fight with my life for her property.'

'What property?' asked Jessica.

'A table. The Comtesse saw it in the drawing room when we were in Maurice's house yesterday. She left some money and marched out with it. She makes the same mistake as your father—she thinks that money will buy her what she wants. And Francine's here to prove that it won't.'

'The table, monsieur, if you please,' came inexorably from Francine.

He looked up at her.

'You're not really angry, are you?' he asked.

'Would you like people to take away your furniture, monsieur?'

'No, of course not, but I'd blame it on the real culprit; I wouldn't take it out of a couple of poor fellows who couldn't hope to control a battle-axe like that. You know battle-axe?'

Francine knew.

'Perhaps you will bring me the table, monsieur. Your friend has the money.'

'You don't imagine, do you,' asked Sebastian, 'that the Comtesse is going to take this quietly? You'll have to argue; you might even have to fight for possession. Do you want our help?'

'I want my table,' said Francine.

'We don't know where it is,' explained Joss. 'It wasn't in the Comtesse's room last night; for all I know, she might have put it with all her other treasures under lock and key.'

'No lock and no key,' said Maurice. 'I went inside.'

'Inside where?' asked Sebastian.

'I went inside lots of rooms. I know where the table is.'

'Then go at once and bring it,' said Francine. 'Take the money and put it on a bureau where she can find it. Go quickly; we must go home to Grandpère. And bring your luggage, but bring the table first.'

Maurice jumped down and ran into the chateau. There was silence for a time after he went; Jessica and Francine were exchanging a long look, seemingly casual, but taking in every detail of dress and appearance. While they studied one another, Joss and Sebastian studied them: the tall, slender Jessica in slacks and sweater; Francine, small and rounded and as fair as the other was dark. The eyes of the two girls met and a smile, slow, enchanting,

140

parted Francine's lips. Jessica's face glowed into sudden friendliness.

'Do you live far away?' she asked.

'Four kilometres,' said Francine. 'Are you staying here?'

'We want her to,' said Sebastian. 'I've just been trying to talk her into it, but she refuses. She says she doesn't like the Comtesse.'

'I, too, I do not like the Comtesse,' said Francine gravely.

There was a slight pause. The two girls glanced at one another and Joss thought that there was an appeal sent and answered.

'If the trains are making difficulties for you,' said Francine slowly, 'we shall be very happy to have you with us, if that would help.'

Jessica gave a deep sigh of relief.

'That would help enormously,' she said. 'Are you quite sure you don't mind?'

'I am quite sure,' smiled Francine.

'Then—' Jessica turned to Sebastian—'if you wouldn't mind bringing down my luggage—'

'We'll both go,' said Joss. 'We'll bring Maurice's, too.'

'Then I'll go in and find the Comtesse,' said Jessica, 'and thank her for putting me up last night.'

'We were counting on having a woman to look after us,' said Sebastian. 'Look, why don't you stay and help us to fix up our rooms? The Comtesse had promised us some furniture; you

141

can help to choose it, if you will. Then we'll drive you over to Francine's in the yellow car. How would that do?'

Jessica was about to say that this would do very well, when there was a loud outcry. Maurice had come out of the chateau at a trot, carrying the table; not far behind him came the Comtesse, showing a surprising turn of speed.

'Come back!' she yelled furiously. 'You! Little boy! Little devil! Come back!'

Maurice came straight on, making for the waggon. As the Comtesse saw it, she halted and stood staring for a time; she was clearly measuring the odds. At last, deciding that they were too heavy, she turned on her heel and went inside.

'Perhaps,' suggested Francine to Jessica, 'it would be better to say good-bye another time?'

'No, I'll get it over now, and then I shan't have to see her again,' said Jessica.

Later, Joss and Sebastian watched the waggon, with Maurice and the two girls, scrunch down the drive and out of sight. Then they went in search of the Comtesse. Failing to find her, they appealed to Léon and learned that she was busy locking the rooms in which the furniture was kept. He offered to lead them there, and they followed him through more empty rooms and along more corridors; Joss, who was collecting corridors, brought his total up to eleven. When they found the Comtesse, Léon left them and they went on to see her

142

standing before a large double door and examining a bunch of keys in her hand. She looked up angrily as they drew near.

'If I could get my hands on that girl d'Arnaud,' she said, 'I would make her sorry that she dared to do that.'

'The money,' Sebastian told her, 'is on the bureau; which bureau, I can't tell you.'

'It is just what one would expect from such people,' said the Comtesse bitterly. 'Protestants! On the eve of St Bartholomew, they did not do their work so well. Protestants! Heretics!'

'Hold on, you're coming a bit near home,' Joss reminded her mildly.

'Two big men,' she said, 'standing there and looking on and doing nothing and allowing people to steal from an old woman. You come to the chateau and take my hospitality and you encourage these people to rob me!'

The challenge was ignored; the Comtesse, longing for battle, could not draw the enemy.

'What do you want with me?' she asked.

'We came to see if you would let us have the furniture for two rooms—two bedrooms,' said Sebastian.

'I was just going to lock it up,' she told him. 'It is very fine, isn't it, when it is necessary to lock the inside doors as well as the outside doors? But what that little devil of a boy can do, my nephew can do also. Come with me; I will show you some things and you can choose

143

what you wish to have.'

She threw open the door. Joss and Sebastian went in and then stood still in astonishment.

They were looking at a collection of tables, chairs, beds, furniture of every kind and style and period and every size from tiny footstools to gargantuan wardrobes. Through this room they could see another and then another, and it did not need a connoisseur's eye to see that every piece was of great value. To Joss, who loved good furniture, who saved up to buy an occasional item for his cottage, this assembly was breath-taking. His plan of helping Sebastian to choose and carry out what they needed was forgotten; instead, he walked slowly through the rooms, picking his way between obstacles, examining first this and then that piece with reverence. The Comtesse followed him, her irritability fading.

'There is nothing, as you see, which is not genuine,' she said. 'Whatever in the chateau was not good, I sold. You are interested in furniture?'

'Yes,' said Joss. 'I don't know much, but I'm learning. This is ... it's staggering.' He looked at her curiously. 'I don't understand,' he said slowly, 'how you ... I mean, couldn't you have this round you, with you? Don't you want to live with it, to see it every day, to enjoy it?'

'If I felt so passionately, would I sell it?' she asked.

'You could use the things until they were

144

sold.'

'To me,' she said, 'they are only money, profit, something that I get because I am more clever than those others who call themselves experts. I am well-known for this. I find out things which others do not know. I discover good furniture as others discover, perhaps, good pictures. Only lately I have found something—a missing piece of furniture which I bought at half its value because even those who owned it did not know what it was and what it was worth. Now come; choose what you want and carry it outside; I am wasting my time here.'

They selected enough to furnish, sparsely, the two rooms they were to occupy, but the scheme no longer seemed to Joss the sensible one he had thought it earlier in the day; it had assumed a dreamlike quality. Nor was the dream a pleasant one. The Comte de Chandillot, whom he had thought of, if he had thought of him at all, as decently interred, now seemed to be disconcertingly present among them. Joss, helping Sebastian to carry out a regal-looking bedstead, had the gruesome impression that the Comte was at his shoulder, helping with the refurnishing of the place he had loved so much. It was a relief when all the things had been assembled outside ready to be taken away.

When the two rooms were ready, the Comtesse came to inspect them.

'They look very nice,' she said. 'Now you will be comfortable. And in return, you cannot refuse to do something for me.'

'What, exactly,' asked Sebastian suspiciously.

'It is nothing, nothing at all. It is only about meals. While you stay with me, you cook for yourselves, isn't it so? And if you have to cook for two, to cook for one more will make no difference, and so I have decided that I will take my meals with you because Léon does not cook well. I should like déjeuner early—shall we say twelve o'clock? And dinner, perhaps, at half-past seven. And please pay attention: I do not eat red meat, because it is not good for me. Veal I can take. But for dinner I do not care for anything except a fowl, perhaps, or partridge; duck also I like, if it is young. Do not shop at Cloisy; only in Lysaine. At Cloisy they will rob you. Now I shall go away because you will wish to buy some things and prepare lunch. Please remember that I like every meal to be ready to the time. Now I shall go away.'

She went away.

CHAPTER EIGHT

Jessica woke the next morning in a small, square room flooded with sunshine; a light breeze came through the wide-open window

146

and brought the scent of jasmine to mingle with the smell of furniture polish. She stirred, thrust a slim leg out from between the covers and wiggled her toes in a shaft of sunlight. She felt relaxed, and grateful for the comforts around her, and lay thinking with compassion of Joss and Sebastian, housed more grandly but far less comfortably at the chateau. Life, she reflected, was scarcely ever fair; she had deceived her father and deserted Hubert and was now enjoying herself in a pale pink house with the d'Arnauds; Joss and Sebastian had looked after a small boy and helped an old lady and were marooned in a deserted chateau with nobody to look after them. Propping herself against the pillows, she hugged her knees and pictured the two men; they would now be getting up and cooking themselves some breakfast, and the Comtesse would come in and eat it all. This lovely sunshine would not penetrate those vast, cold rooms. They would hear nothing except the echo of their own voices; there would be none of the pleasant murmuring that rose to her ears from the busy household below.

She rose, bathed and dressed and went downstairs. From the window of the landing she caught sight of Maurice at play with a group of companions in the field adjoining the garden. Like them, he wore an enveloping pinafore; like them, he looked typically and unmistakably French. She smiled, and the smile became warmer as she looked down into the hall and saw Monsieur d'Arnaud. He looked up and saw her, bowed and went on with unhurried steps to his sitting room on the ground floor.

He was a small, spare man, grey-haired, rather frail-looking, with a pointed beard and courtly manners. He spoke no English. He passed his days in his sitting room, which opened on to the garden; he took his lunch there, not far from the tree under which, in fine weather, the other members of the family ate. He could hear their chatter, but he took no part in it; he looked removed, remote. At dinner, he took his place at the head of the table out on the terrace, saying little, but answering remarks addressed to him in his dry, thin voice. Jessica had passed few words with him on the previous night, but she had seen his eyes, dark, keen, resting upon her many times during the meal.

She ran down the stairs and found Francine at work in the kitchen; she smiled as Jessica came in, asked her if she had slept well, placed hot croissants and coffee on a tray and carried it out to the terrace. Jessica sat down with a sigh of happiness, but she did not ask Francine to stay and talk to her as she ate; she had learned already that the routine of the household flowed like a deep, wide river, on and on, smoothly and strongly; visitors, expected or unexpected, were absorbed like tributaries into the main stream and borne on without a pause.

From morning to evening, Francine worked, quietly and serenely, pursuing contentedly a routine that was as well planned as it was long established. Céline came each day and washed and scrubbed and polished, needing no direction, following a well-worn track. The house shone. Sometimes the smell of polish gave way to a delicious smell of hot bread or coffee. Meals were simple, superbly cooked by Francine and served on snowy tablecloths on the table under the tree or on the terrace. Jessica followed her hostess as she worked, and tried to give unobtrusive help where she thought it was needed, but found herself stopping every now and then to enjoy the pictures of neatness and orderliness that greeted her everywhere. She liked to watch Francine, neat in a freshly ironed dress and businesslike apron, sleeves rolled up to her dimpled elbows and her small hands twinkling over her tasks. Francine made no attempt to entertain her; there was an unspoken but frank statement that a house must be run, and well run, and that much of the welcome to guests consisted of keeping the house running well for their benefit. So Jessica watched the cleaning, the cooking and saw the great hampers of wet or dry washing, the hot or cold pies and pastries, and Francine enjoyed having her in the kitchen, sniffing the varied but always delightful smells and talking about the events that had led up to her arrival at the chateau.

'But what I do not see,' she said as she and Jessica discussed the subject, 'is why you have a wedding dress in your luggage.' She gave Jessica a smile, half apology, half teasing. 'You see, Maurice saw it, and he saw other things, too; he told me about them, so I cannot help knowing. He told me that you came in the green car—but I do not understand how this was.'

'I was going to be married,' said Jessica, 'to the Comtesse's nephew.'

Francine's hands became still for a surprised moment.

'To Hubert?'

'Yes. Do you know him?'

'Of course. We all know him; was he not brought up here?'

'Here?' Jessica's voice was high with surprise.

'At the chateau. He lived there until he was nineteen and then his aunt turned him out. In a way,' said Francine judicially, 'I do not blame her. And yet my father says that she could have done more for him.'

'Do you know him well?'

'Very well. We played together as children. She could not prevent it; in the school holidays, he used to come here often. She hates us because we are not Catholics, but she could not tie Hubert up with a rope. When he was

150

nineteen, he was sent away, but he has come back sometimes, and I have seen him. But he does not go to the chateau.' She studied the other girl gravely for a few moments. 'You are in love with him?'

'No! Oh no!'

'But if you were going to marry him—?'

Jessica embarked upon an explanation. She began haltingly, but under Francine's gentle and sympathetic gaze found herself pouring out the facts which related not only to Hubert, but also to the strained relations which had for so long existed between her father and herself. She thought of Monsieur d'Arnaud and wondered whether a touch of his imperturbability might not have improved her own father—and then thrust the thought aside. She had been, she was aware, a far from dutiful daughter.

She brought her narrative to an end, and Francine gave a little sigh.

'You left him,' she asked, 'at St Malo?'

'Yes.'

Francine shook her head slowly.

'Poor Hubert,' she said softly. 'Of course, it is what he deserved, and yet ... how is it his fault? He told you, I suppose, that the money should be his?'

'Yes. By rights, was his expression. And the chateau, he said, was his too—by rights.'

'The chateau was left to him, but the Comtesse can live in it for her lifetime. It would

151

have been better, perhaps, to say that Hubert should live there for his lifetime. Then the Comtesse would not have been able to send him away.'

'Why wasn't the furniture left to him, too?'

'Because when the Comte died, all the furniture belonged to the Comtesse. It is difficult to see who is right and who is wrong. The Comte spent all his money on the chateau. When he died, the Comtesse said that to live, she must become a furniture dealer, and that is what she is now. When Hubert's parents died, she gave him a home and some sort of education, but she gave him nothing to do, nothing to occupy himself—and then she said to him: Earn for yourself. When he said that he could not, she said to him: Go. You can see that in this way, Hubert has been unfortunate? If she had allowed him to earn money doing the only thing he could do, the thing which she herself had taught him—judging furniture, choosing furniture, buying and selling furniture—but she did not give him the chance.'

There was a thoughtful pause.

'In some ways,' said Jessica at last, 'I'm sorry I didn't leave him the car.'

'You do not know—' Francine's eyes were narrowed in speculation—'anything about the sale? Anything about what Hubert was to buy there?'

'A screen, he said.'

152

'A screen. It is interesting that for this screen she did something so strange, something she must of all things have wanted not to do—give Hubert the money. It must have been a very important screen. I shall ask my father if he has heard about it; he will know. And who,' she went on after a pause, 'are the two Englishmen who came to the chateau with the Comtesse?'

'They couldn't get their car off the boat, and they drove her down here. She bought no less than two cars on the way.'

'That would not surprise anybody here. She will argue with a shopkeeper over three francs, but to get to a sale, she will hire a car from Cloisy and drive across France if it is somewhere that the trains are not convenient. The two Englishmen live in Jersey? Of course; otherwise they could not have brought Maurice.'

'Only one of them brought him.'

'The quiet one?'

'Yes. Joss Armstrong. The other one's called Sebastian Page. He's Lord Willburn's son. I put him down, at first, as rich, idle and conceited, but I'm beginning to think that perhaps he's only rich and idle.'

Francine smiled.

'With you, he will not be conceited for long.' She nodded towards a basket that stood, covered with a clean napkin, on the dresser. 'In that basket I have put some things for them to eat. It is a pity that they have to cook for

153

themselves. And I owe them something for their kindness to Maurice.'

Jessica walked over and peered into the hamper.

'What's inside?'

'Some pies; some tarts with honey; some new bread and a cold chicken. I will send it with Maurice and—'

'Oh no! Don't send it! Don't, please,' begged Jessica. 'If you send it, don't you know what'll happen? The Comtesse'll help herself to the lion's share. She eats like a horse, the pig. If you send it, Joss and Sebastian will just sit there watching her wolf it.'

'Then how? Shall they go hungry because the Comtesse is so many animals?'

'Let them come and eat it here,' begged Jessica. 'Please! Why should they feed her? Let them come here and they can eat it out of doors—out in the garden, like a picnic. They can—But it's your house,' she ended lamely.

'No, it is my father's house,' smiled Francine. 'He will be glad to return their kindness, so if you think that they would like to come, then certainly ask them. If they wish to eat here every day, lunch and dinner, it will be no trouble.'

'You ... you mean that?'

'Of course.'

'Then I'll go and ask them now, before you've got time to change your mind. Oh Francine, I'm so grateful to you! I was feeling

154

so sorry for them! I'll go and tell them—and I promise to see that they don't cadge.'

'Cadge? I do not know that word.'

'Then I'll see that they don't teach it to you. Au revoir.'

'You are going to walk so far?'

'It's nothing. A couple of miles. I'll go across the fields.'

She walked first to Cloisy and glanced into the shops to satisfy herself that the two men were not in them buying provisions; then she crossed the fields, walked over the bridge and through the woods, entering the chateau grounds by a small wooden door in the encircling wall. From the door, a path led through shrubberies to the great grey building.

She had almost reached it when a sound made her leap aside. It was a hiss, and while she did not expect to find dangerous snakes in the chateau grounds, she felt it wise to jump first and investigate afterwards.

Investigation revealed nothing on the path before or behind her. She walked on a few steps and then the sound came again, this time close and unmistakable.

'Psst!'

The bushes on her left parted; a bewhiskered face peered out at her. Without hesitation, Jessica took to her heels and ran. She was alone and out of sight of the chateau windows; she was not of a nervous disposition, but being hissed at by suspicious-looking characters with bristling moustaches was not an experience she cared for.

Fleet though she was, the footsteps on the path behind her were fleeter; she was beginning to be touched by real alarm when her name came pantingly from her pursuer.

'Jessica! Jessica!'

She stopped at once, her fears at an end. Only one person of her acquaintance called her 'Jayzeeker.' Turning, she surveyed with astonishment the figure now creeping furtively back into the bushes.

'Hubert!' she called sharply.

The whiskers, the luxuriant moustache turned for a panic-stricken moment in her direction.

'Ssh! Be careful, I beg! If I am caught—' said Hubert.

'If you're caught looking like that, your aunt will call the police first and identify you afterwards,' said Jessica. 'What are you doing here?'

'I wished to speak with you. I had to speak with you,' said Hubert from the protection of the bushes. 'You went away so suddenly, I could not explain some things.'

'You explained everything,' said Jessica. 'Where on earth did you get those props?'

'Props?'

'Never mind. My advice to you is to go away before your aunt comes snooping.'

'I will go in a few moments,' said Hubert.

'But you should not have left me at St Malo before I could say these things.'

'What things?'

'Many things. First of all, that I loved you, Jessica. I really loved you,' Hubert assured her earnestly.

'Next thing?' enquired Jessica.

'That you were rich, that I knew. In my position, it was not possible that I should love a girl who was poor. But when you say that I was going to pay for the car with your money, there you were wrong.'

'There *you* were wrong,' corrected Jessica. 'Next thing?'

'What I was going to do, was to marry you—for love, naturally.'

'Naturally.'

'And when we were married, I would have said to my aunt: Look, here is my wife, it is fitting that she should come to live at the chateau and—'

'At *this* chateau?' asked Jessica incredulously. 'You mean this—'

'You have not seen it to advantage. She has neglected it. She has robbed it of its furniture. If you could have seen it as it was once, with curtains, with tables and chairs and with beautiful pictures and chandeliers—'

'I've seen enough—with two candles,' said Jessica.

'But it is beautiful! Look at it! It is beyond words beautiful,' said Hubert passionately. 'If you brought to our marriage money, did I not bring in time this beautiful chateau, the home of my forebearers? You think that I planned only to get something, but I planned to give also—to give you this home, to ask my aunt to return to us some furniture, to—'

'It's no use,' said Jessica, not ungently. 'It's all over, Hubert, and I don't think you ought to risk hanging about here, even in that disguise.'

'There is no disguise, except to hide my face from my aunt,' said Hubert. 'But there is another thing to say.'

'Well, what is it?'

'Shall I not have the car?' asked Hubert piteously. 'It is locked away, but if you got the keys from Léon, or if you took them away when nobody was looking, you could so easily—'

'No, I couldn't,' said Jessica firmly. 'Besides, I'm not even staying here.'

'But you are! Yesterday in the morning, I arrived and I saw you! I looked through the windows and I saw you in the kitchen and—'

'Your aunt gave me a room for one night. If you call it a room. It was right on the top of a tower.'

'You would not believe it, but that is where my aunt kept me,' said Hubert.

'Your mistake was in letting her keep you at all,' said Jessica. 'You should have gone out and ... and done something.'

'But that is what I did! I found a beautiful
158

girl to marry me and—But where are you staying?'

'At Cloisy, with Francine d'Arnaud.'

'With them! But they are my friends! If you are there, I can see you, visit you, speak with you! That place, I assure you, is one which is the last that my aunt would visit! But Francine and I, we are friends from long ago. She is beautiful, though not as beautiful as you. Often, in the past, I have said to myself that if only she had money, and would be a Catholic, I would marry her. I am glad that you are with her.'

'How did you get here?' asked Jessica.

'From St Malo? First of all I—' He broke off to gaze reproachfully at her. 'That was not kind, Jessica, to take the car. If I had had the car, I would not have minded so much anything else. But you took it, and I had no way of following. Then I telephoned to René and Carla and told them that I had missed you in some way, and they telephoned to some friends they have near St Malo, and they came to find me and they drove me to some friends of theirs near Cloisy, and they left me there. These friends are very kind to me; I told them that my aunt had taken away my car, and they are very sympathetic. They have asked me to stay with them until things have arranged themselves better with me.'

'Well, you'd better go back to them,' advised Jessica.

'But the car, Jessica? You could bring it to me?'

'No, Hubert.'

'You could tell my aunt that I wish to sell it and bring the money to her?'

'No, Hubert.'

'It is a pity,' sighed Hubert. 'I will go now, and I will come to Cloisy to see you.'

The bushes met and hid him from view. Jessica walked on, and after vainly endeavouring to get an answer to her ringing, walked into the Chateau and found Joss and Sebastian in the kitchen, moodily regarding their preparations for lunch.

'I've got an invitation from Francine,' she said without preamble. 'Meals at her house every day. Lunch and dinner.'

The kitchen knife dropped from Sebastian's hands and he stood looking at her with deep affection.

'Thank God,' he said. 'That's an answer to prayer, and you're a girl in a million. Joss and I were standing here wondering how we could work it.'

'I've worked it for you,' said Jessica. 'Coming?'

'Just as soon as I've told Léon to tell the Comtesse that I've told him to tell her that from now on, she can fix her own meals. Joss, you can make him a present of those stores we bought. Jessica, how did you come? In the fancy waggon?'

'I walked through the woods, like who was it in the fairy story, and guess who walked on in the wolf's part?'

'Not Hubert?' asked Joss.

'Yes. With false moustaches.'

'If he's going to hang round here, I shall say a few words to him,' said Sebastian.

'You'll leave him alone,' said Jessica.

He looked down at her in surprise.

'The moustaches must have been elegant,' he commented. 'They seem to have won your heart. Do you want him hanging about?'

'No. If there's any talking to be done, I'll do it,' she said. 'It doesn't take heavy ammunition to deal with poor Hubert. Come on, let's hurry.'

They walked together to Cloisy. At the gate of *Marielle*, the two men stood looking over the gate for a few moments, and then Sebastian gave a long, happy sigh. The table was covered with a huge white cloth; Maurice, in his pinafore, was setting the last of the glasses and putting a fresh white napkin at each place. Céline was coming out of the house with two large bottles of wine. In the doorway, Francine stood, cool and composed, her eyes checking the table arrangements, her hands untying the strings of her apron. At the door of his sitting room, Monsieur d'Arnaud stood bowing gravely.

'For what we are about to receive—' Sebastian pushed open the gate and ushered

Jessica and Joss into the garden—'we are already truly thankful.'

CHAPTER NINE

From the moment of sitting down to the open-air lunch in the garden of *Marielle*, Joss and Sebastian understood that their holiday was to run, after all, along very agreeable lines. The change from the chateau to the low, rambling pink house was a removal from cheerlessness to comfort, from the sombre to the sunlit. On the previous night at the chateau, when they had slept in the huge rooms whose shadows seemed to harbour the long-dead denizens of Chandillot—that, said Sebastian, might have had an appeal for the more imaginative Joss, but for himself, he would rather have been camping in the middle of Salisbury Plain. Joss made no comment on the unaccustomed procedure of going to bed by candlelight, but like Sebastian, he felt that there were other things he would have enjoyed more. The late Comte de Chandillot had more than once peered at him from the other side of the wavering candle, and a gentleman with long curls had appeared from behind a particularly good piece of furniture; he could only suppose that it was Louis Quinze.

'It was my idea to stay on and persuade the

Comtesse to furnish us a couple of rooms,' admitted Sebastian, 'but it was one of my rare slip-ups in judgment and if hadn't been for Francine, the days would have been as gloomy as the nights. God bless Francine.'

He and Joss observed, as Jessica had done, that their presence did not disturb the serene routine of the household. They caused no stir and no disorder. Céline gave them a wide, friendly grin; Francine made them welcome and went on with her work; Monsieur d'Arnaud expressed his pleasure at seeing them, and retired to his sitting room, where the greater part of his days were passed. He seemed to enjoy, in his withdrawn way, the addition of the two men to the company at *Marielle*. He walked out at dusk to the dinner table set on the terrace near his room, and took his place at the head, bowing to the others as they waited for him, motioning them to their places and bending his head to murmur a grace. Joss, taking his seat at the candlelit board, thought of his own dinners in Jersey, which he ate from a tray balanced on the window sill of his sitting room. He looked round at this widely contrasted scene and found delight stirring in him. He watched the faces of Francine and Jessica, always lovely but infinitely more lovely in the dancing candlelight, with the velvet hangings of the night behind them. He enjoyed as in a dream the leisurely pace of the meal, the perfection of the food, the orchestra of voices;

Sebastian's deep tones, Monsieur d'Arnaud's light ones; Francine's low and calm, Jessica's swift and staccato. He listened to Monsieur d'Arnaud's brief, occasional, informed comment, saying little himself, for he was lost in appreciation of the scene and perhaps even more of the food. Only when the name of the Comtesse came up did he address a direct question to his host.

'Why does she live as she does—so shabbily?' he asked.

'The Comtesse?' Monsieur d'Arnaud's long white hands seemed to hold the question while he deliberated his reply. 'Who knows. She does not give reasons for what she does. She is an eccentric.'

'She told us—' Joss, whose French stopped some way short of fluency, paused to gather the words together—'she told us that the Comte had spent all her money on the chateau.'

'That is only half true. He spent some of it, perhaps, but not all. She is not the woman,' said Monsieur d'Arnaud with his faint, sardonic smile, 'to stand aside and let herself be totally impoverished.'

'How long,' asked Sebastian, 'has she lived like that—in one room?'

'It has been a gradual change. While her husband lived, there was of course order, dignity; there were servants and a certain amount of comfort, even of style. But this cost a great deal of money, and at his death she was

164

not prepared to pay any more for the upkeep of a place that she had never liked. Year by year, there was less; fewer servants, more empty rooms, a greater attention to expenditure. She does not understand, I think, how far she has fallen from the old dignity. Or perhaps she does not care. Money: this has become her life. How to gain, how to save, how to amass money.'

'But her nephew said—' began Jessica, and then paused as Monsieur d'Arnaud's dark eyes came to rest on her. He seemed to be weighing her words against what his niece had told him of the affair between Hubert and herself.

'Ah, her nephew!' he said at last, and there was a smile behind his eyes. 'You are interested in what he says, mademoiselle?'

'He told me a lot about his aunt.'

'What he says, in all probability, mademoiselle, would be only half the truth. They are very different, those two, but in some ways you find that they are alike.'

'What is the truth?' asked Sebastian.

'The truth? You would say, what are the facts?' asked Monsieur in turn. 'The facts are that the chateau became, in the minds of those who owned it, a symbol. It represented a grandeur, a way of life which they could no longer afford but which they could not bring themselves to give up. That is one fact. Then there is the fact that for years, for perhaps half a century, money has been poured out in the

165

attempt to run, to repair or to restore the chateau. The Comtesse—the one of whom we speak—could do nothing to control the expenditure while her husband was alive, and so since his death she has perhaps been making up for lost time. I can remember her when she first came to Lysaine. She was, you would not believe it, very handsome.'

There was silence; polite, but of complete disbelief. Monsieur d'Arnaud shrugged and continued.

'She tried to persuade the Comte that they should try to gather money instead of spending it; she proposed that they should buy and sell fine furniture. But the Comte, having bought a fine piece, could not be persuaded to part with it. So at last the Comtesse began to buy for herself, and that is why, when he died, he could not leave any furniture to his nephew— because the Comtesse owned it all. So Hubert Ramage inherited the chateau and nothing but the chateau, and even that he cannot have, because the Comtesse has turned him out.'

'And that is wrong,' came firmly and unexpectedly from Francine.

'Wrong? Right? How can you judge?' asked her father.

'She should have done something with him.'

'She should have attempted it, perhaps.'

'Then yes; she should have attempted it.'

'Why?' asked Sebastian. 'She educated him; why shouldn't he be able to earn a living just

166

like anybody else?'

'Like you, for example?' asked Joss with a grin.

'That's beside the point. We're talking about Hubert, and it seems to me that all he's after is money without the bore of earning it. In that, at least, I'm on the Comtesse's side.'

'And I am on Hubert's,' said Francine. 'He grew up with her, and for all those years she despised him and made no secret of it. She expected him always to be weak, and so he became weak. And having made him weak, she should not have given him so much money to buy the screen.'

'That is true,' said her father.

'And I am glad that she did not get it,' ended Francine.

'There is a sale next week at La Rochelle,' said Monsieur d'Arnaud. 'I think that you will find the Comtesse there.'

'She'll probably ask us to drive her there,' said Sebastian.

'Then I would do so,' advised Monsieur d'Arnaud. 'You will find it interesting. The sale will be held at the house of the Marquis de Moelle; the house is beautiful and in it there are many lovely things. You should go. And now, if you will excuse me—'

He rose and gave a stiff little bow and walked into the house. The others were left in the light of the candles. Céline poured more wine into the two men's glasses; they looked across the table at the two girls and the Comtesse and her affairs were forgotten.

'It's a wonderful night,' said Sebastian. 'Francine, what do you do on lovely moonlight nights?'

'The same as I do on other nights,' said Francine in her tranquil way. 'I sew, I read, I mend, I play cards with my father, I write letters.'

'Do you ever leave Cloisy?' asked Joss.

'Sometimes. My father and I go to visit our relations.'

Joss looked at her. She looked milk-white in the candlelight; her hair shone. Jessica seemed all shadow, this girl all light. A lovely pair, he mused, and knew that Sebastian was thinking the same.

'Let's walk,' said Sebastian suddenly. 'It's only a three-quarter moon, but it'll look nice on the river. Coming?'

He held out a hand to Jessica, who was beside him. She rose, and the two walked slowly through the garden and out into the lane. Joss followed with Francine; they strolled easily and did not bother to catch up with the others. Joss found nothing to say, but he was aware that, unlike other occasions on which he found himself alone with an attractive girl, his lack of conversation produced no restlessness in his companion. Francine seemed lost in pleasant little dreams of her own; Joss, glancing down at her presently, thought he could see a smile on her lips.

'Are you smiling?' he asked.

'Yes.'

'Private joke?'

'Not private, and not a joke,' said Francine gently. 'I was thinking that people are interesting. You and your friend. You are both ... quite different.'

'I suppose we are. I suppose, in a way, that's why we're friends,' said Joss.

'You have known each other for long?'

'It isn't one of those old-school-friend associations. We met as men and not as boys. Sometimes I wonder why it's lasted as long as it has. Sebastian leads rather a gay life; he moves fast, and people who move fast don't always feel inclined to stop and wait for the slower ones.'

'You are the slower one?'

'Most definitely.'

'Perhaps he likes to meet you often because you are restful?'

He was uncertain whether this was a question or a statement, and if a statement, whether he liked being referred to as restful when he was walking in the moonlight with a pretty girl.

'Sebastian works in England?' she asked.

'If you call it working. When the subject comes up, and he can't dodge round it, he says Stock Exchange and lets it go at that. He's got two estates to look after—one in Yorkshire and the other in Kent; I think he'd make a good job of running them if they weren't already being run very efficiently by stewards or managers or agents. But his real work is dodging determined mothers. He's a good catch, matrimonially, and they work at it all the year round.'

'He doesn't want to get married?'

Joss hesitated. For a man who wished to avoid the shoals of matrimony, Sebastian did some remarkably dangerous sailing.

'I don't know,' he said at last. 'I think that when a man's very much sought after, dodging becomes almost a career. After a time, he forgets that he ought to be settling down, or perhaps he never gets a chance to make a free choice. Even the nicest girls seem to have ambitious mothers. A man like Sebastian, when you come to look at it, has a lot to offer mothers: looks, money, a title and a long pedigree. It all adds up to make him a pretty good proposition. He's hunted—there's no other word for it—and whether a man's hunted because he's a prize or because he's a pest makes very little difference, he has to keep on the run. One way and another, I think Sebastian stands up to the life pretty well.'

'You like him very much?'

This, clearly, was a statement.

'Yes, I suppose I do.'

Her face was upturned; her glance rested on him for a few moments. Joss knew that she was studying him and knew, too—and felt a glow of gratitude at the realization—that there was nothing of disappointment in the scrutiny. She liked him; how he knew, he could not have told, but he was familiar with the long, narrowed look that girls gave him, a look that bored through him and told him that he had not come up to expectations. He had only to watch Sebastian, he had told himself more than once, to know what girls liked; they liked firm handling, firm embraces and firm offers, and they found his own slow ways and slower conversation boring. This girl was the first, in his experience, who did not indicate clearly that she would rather have been paired with Sebastian. An absurd desire to thank her rose in him, and he fought it down. If he was beginning to become a success at last, he reminded himself with an inward grin, he must learn to accept the facts, as Sebastian did, as his due.

'It's odd,' he said, 'to think that you've often been across to Jersey.'

'To see my sister? That is not strange, surely?'

'Well, strange to think that we didn't meet.'

'You like living there?'

'Very much. Is Maurice's father a Jerseyman?'

'Yes. He and my sister have been married for ten years. She is twelve years older than I am.'

'Have you always lived here in Cloisy?'

'We came here when I was a year old. My father bought the house for my mother—*Marielle*. She was delicate, and it is healthy here in Cloisy, but she died soon after we came.'

'Do you ever leave your father?'

'Yes, of course. When I am away, Céline looks after him well, and we have friends here in Cloisy who see that he is not lonely.'

He tried to think of her in a different setting, and found it difficult; she seemed to belong to the peace and the quiet of this place. He wondered who her friends were; he had not seen anybody here who could have been a companion for her.

He had not thought of turning homeward, and was surprised when the voices of Jessica and Sebastian came out of the darkness.

'Going back already?' he asked them.

'Yes,' said Jessica. 'I'm sleepy. I don't know whether it's the air, or Francine's food, or the wine or Sebastian's conversation; I just want to sleep.'

They strolled back together, easy and relaxed. At the gate of the house, the two girls went in and the men turned to walk back to the chateau.

'Well—' Sebastian spoke out of a long silence—'it's going to be a good holiday.'

'Yes. We've been lucky,' said Joss. 'If there'd been nothing but the Comtesse and the chateau, I don't suppose we'd have enjoyed it

172

much. As it is—'

'As it is?' prompted Sebastian.

'Well, as I said, we've been lucky. Early nights, good healthy walks, wonderful French food, good wine.'

'And?'

'Well, and two very nice girls.'

'Some people,' commented Sebastian, 'would put first things first, but not you. All the same, you're right and we're lucky. All we've got to do now is try to keep our heads.'

'How d'you mean, keep our heads?'

'I mean just what I say. You've just enumerated all the things that a kind fate has provided; now you've got to go further and try to assess what effect soft night air, good food, good wine and two lovely women have on two susceptible men.'

'I'm not—'

'—susceptible? That's what you think. The fact is that you've never—at least, never since I've known you—been in a situation quite like this.'

'I don't see any situation,' said Joss.

'You will. You and I,' said Sebastian, 'are in a very dangerous position.'

'You might be, but I can name at least a dozen girls you've known much longer than two weeks without showing any sign of losing your head.'

'The danger in the present situation,' said Sebastian, 'can be summed up in the one word:

propinquity. You can meet girls off and on, and that's safe enough, because the interval between the off and the on gives you enough time to remember what you said last time and to decide what you'll say next. In other words, when you're on-and-offing, you can snatch just enough time to glance at a compass. But for the next two weeks, we're going to see two outstandingly pretty girls morning, noon and pretty far into the night. We're going to see them against a very attractive background and in some remarkably potent settings—I hadn't realized, before, how heady candlelight could be. I'm telling you this tonight because I don't want you to come to me next week, or the week after, and set up a howl because I didn't put the thing before you clearly. I don't know what your views on marrying are—I haven't checked up on them for some time—but I remember your telling me some time ago that you'd like to find a wife.'

'Of course I'd like a wife,' said Joss. 'But I'd need a lot more than two weeks before I knew a girl well enough to know whether we'd suit one another or not. I'm not like you; I like to go at a thing slowly. Which is more, as the Comtesse says, I refuse to believe that two reasonably decent men can't see two nice girls for two weeks without coming up against what you call a situation. We can all be good friends, can't we?'

'In any other circumstances, yes. In these,

no. And so if I were you,' advised Sebastian, 'I'd tell myself that this was probably the finest opportunity you'll ever have of getting yourself a perfect wife. The same goes for me. And I think we've made a good start. What did you and Francine talk about on the walk just now?'

'About you.'

'Well, that's not exactly progress, but I think she likes you. And if the look on your face at dinner was anything to go by, you like her too.'

'Who wouldn't? She's the kindest girl I ever met. But—'

'But what?'

'A lot of girls like me. That is, they don't actively dislike me. And that's as far as it ever goes.'

'That's as far as it has gone in the past. Now you're going to find out what happens when you stage it with moonlight and candlelight and good food and *vin du pays*.'

'Well, speaking for myself—'

'You needn't speak for yourself,' said Sebastian. 'What I've said goes for you and for me, too. For both of us. It goes, in fact, for all men. These are probably the last sensible remarks I shall ever address to you. Next time we walk through these woods, shall I be discussing coldly? No. I'll be throwing leaves over myself, and tripping along by your side and chanting that old song:

"Amo, amas, I love a lass,

As a cedar tall and slender."

How does it go on?'

  '"Sweet cowslip's grace
  Is her nom'native case,
  And she's of the feminine gender,"'

supplied Joss.
'Yes. She's of the feminine gender,' said
Sebastian. 'So think over what's coming.'
Joss had no reply to make; there was
something in the words, or in the conviction
with which they were spoken, that silenced
him.
Wordless, they walked on in the darkness,
staring thoughtfully ahead. The branches
above them stirred and spoke to them softly.

  'Amo, amas, I love a lass...'

CHAPTER TEN

Hubert arrived at *Marielle* on the following
morning.
He came without his disguise. He opened the
gate and stood looking uncertainly at
Sebastian, who was sitting on a long wicker
chair in the garden, enjoying the sunshine and
the knowledge that lunch was being prepared.
176

He looked up at the visitor and gave an exclamation of surprise.

'Well, now!' he said.

Hubert advanced cautiously.

'You know me, perhaps?' he asked.

'Of course; you're the chap with the green car.'

Hubert looked down at his dusty shoes and sighed.

'The car I no longer have. Now I have to walk,' he said. 'Have you left the chateau?'

'Only for meals. Where have you come from?'

'From my friends, who do not live far away. They are looking after me. Yesterday I waited for Jessica—I thought that she was staying at the chateau, but when she said that she was here, I knew that it would be no longer necessary for me to exercise caution. It was only for my aunt—Has my aunt spoken of me?'

'Only to say that if she sees you anywhere near the chateau, she'll call the police. I think she means it.'

'I am sure that she means it. May I sit on this chair for a few moments beside you?'

'Hadn't you better go in and announce yourself first?'

'Yes. No. Perhaps. I will do it in a moment, but there are things I wish to ask you first.' Hubert lowered himself thankfully into the chair, stretched out his legs and brushed the dust from his trousers. 'It is hot to walk,' he said. 'My friends have a car, but they have not put it at my disposal. Their house is not very large, not very comfortable, but it is convenient for me at the present time.'

'What exactly have you come for?' asked Sebastian. 'I mean, wouldn't it be wiser, in the circumstances, to keep well away from Cloisy, or from Lysaine?'

'From Lysaine, certainly, but my aunt does not come often to Cloisy, and if she did, she would not come to this house; Francine and her father are Protestants and she hates all Protestants, French Protestants above all. I know Francine from long ago; she will be happy to see me. I wish to speak about something to her father; it is very important. I also wish to see Jessica.'

'I gathered that Jessica—' Sebastian paused.

'—is angry with me? Yes. She does not understand. I have come to say some things to her. Perhaps now that she has seen what kind of woman my aunt is, she will understand more clearly why I acted in that way. You have seen the chateau; you have seen what my aunt has done there, how she lives in one room like a peasant? The chateau is not hers; it is mine, but stupidly, my uncle allowed that she should stay there for her life. Her life? She will live forever. Certainly she will live until I am an old man.'

'But—I'm sorry to sound unduly curious—if there's no money, do you propose to—?'

'To live there? She has turned me out. But if she would have me again, I would not wish to use the whole; no, in that I am wiser than my uncle and those who went before him. I understand that it is impossible. All I wish to do, all I hope to do, all I mean to do when my aunt is dead is to preserve a little—a quarter, one wing. It is my home!' declared Hubert, rocking the chair with his passion. 'I am not of the name of de Chandillot, but I am the only one left of their blood. It is not to be grand, you understand, that I say I shall live at the chateau. If you give me a chateau now, this minute, another chateau, any other chateau, I shall refuse to take it. I do not want any chateau. I wish only to live in the chateau that my uncle left to me. Do you think, when he said that she could live there for her life, he imagined for one moment that she would turn me out? No. He thought only that she would keep some rooms for herself and give me the others. Otherwise, it is a farce! She is there, in that whole place, needing only one room. I am where? Nowhere. Is this right? Is this just?'

'What do you think Jessica can do about it?' asked Sebastian.

'She can forgive me because I deceived her a little. She can marry me, if she will. You can see how it is? I have a home, but I am homeless; with a wife who has also money, I can persuade my aunt to permit us to live at the chateau. She can then—Please,' he begged, 'will you go and

179

say to Francine that I am here? Francine is kind; she will help me. She will talk to Jessica and then it will be all right.'

Sebastian rose and went indoors; following the sounds of activity, he went into the kitchen; Francine and Joss were working and Jessica was watching.

'There's a visitor outside,' he announced.

Francine turned from the table and looked at him.

'For me?' she asked.

'It's Hubert,' he said.

'Then it will be for Jessica.'

'He wants to see you,' said Sebastian.

'Tell him to go away, Francine,' pleaded Jessica. 'I saw him yesterday and told him that it was no good. Tell him I'm sorry. Tell him that more than half of it was my fault and I'm really very, very sorry, but I don't want to go on arguing about it. And if he keeps appearing at Cloisy, his aunt will see him or get to hear of it, and then there'll be trouble. Tell him to go away and stay away.'

'Why don't you go out and talk to him?' Sebastian asked her suddenly, and Jessica stared at him in surprise.

'Why should I?' she asked.

'I don't quite know,' said Sebastian, 'but my feeling is that somebody will have to do something. The chap seems to have come to a sort of dead end; he's made his big plunge and got himself into deeper water than he
180

bargained for and he's ... he's floundering. He's lost his fighting spirit, such as it was. I don't want to harrow your feelings, but there's something pathetic about him. His shoes, perhaps. Covered in dust. He didn't have any dust on his shoes at St Malo; while he was never my type, there was something spruce about him. If a man who'd just pinched a lot of money could be said to look self-respecting, then he did. Now he doesn't. He doesn't look like a man any more, he looks about eighteen, and lost. Forlorn. He came in at the gate just now looking as though he was going to pass the hat round.'

'Perhaps he is,' suggested Joss.

'I will go and see him.' Francine was untying her apron.

'I'll come, too,' said Jessica. 'If I stay here, Sebastian will have us all howling in misery.'

Sebastian opened the door for them and looked at Joss when they had gone.

'I suppose I sounded like a Scot giving off a dirge on the bagpipes,' he said, 'but I only said what I thought. The fellow's lost all his starch. Remember how debonair he looked? Now he just looks dismal.'

'Perhaps he was really in love.'

'No. He's not lovelorn; he's frightened. I daresay he's brought off one or two mildly shady deals in his time, but he obviously isn't cut out for anything requiring real nerve. He's got himself into a mess, and he's waiting for someone to get him out of it. He was a fool to give the Comtesse an excuse for being really mean.'

Jessica, looking at Hubert with a mixture of sympathy and exasperation, had just told him the same thing.

'And now you've let her get into a really strong position,' she said.

'With me,' said Hubert frankly, 'she was always in a strong position. I was frightened of her, and this is not from cowardice, but only because she made violent scenes and then I became frightened. If you will marry me, everything will be different; you will be able to stand before me.'

'If I marry anybody,' said Jessica, 'it won't be to provide them with a screen from violent aunts.'

'Do not mention screens,' begged Hubert. 'The screen was the cause of everything, everything.' His voice broke. 'I am without a home and without money; even I am going to ask Francine to give me some food. You can see what the screen has done for me.'

'You must stay to lunch,' said Francine.

'You are very kind,' said Hubert. 'Afterwards, perhaps I may be permitted to see your father? But not before eating, because I am very hungry. My friends do not eat well.'

'There is a herb omelette, and veal, salad and cheese.'

'You are an angel.'

'But before lunch, you had better wash. I will take you upstairs,' said Francine. 'After lunch we shall talk about what is to be done.'

She led him into the house; Sebastian, coming out a few moments later, found Jessica staring moodily over the gate.

'Where is he?' he asked.

'Upstairs being washed and got ready for lunch.'

He leaned on the gate beside her and looked at her curiously.

'What made you do it?' he asked.

'Do what?'

'Say you'd marry the poor fellow.'

She turned to him impatiently.

'I wish you'd stop this poor-fellow, poor-fellowing,' she said. 'He's a coward and a weakling and you know it.'

'Well, of course,' he agreed amiably. 'One can see at a glance. So what made you think that he'd make good husband material?'

'Oh ...' Jessica walked to one of the wicker chairs, sat down and leaned back wearily. 'I don't know. Yes, I do know. It seems silly now, when we know all about his aunt and the money and the way he used it, but in June, in Jersey ... well, he was different.'

'He was the same, but you didn't lift up the lid and look.'

'Why should I? He was presentable, he was nice to look at; going out with him was fun. You can laugh if you like, but when he's not being frightened out of his life, he's got a ... a sort of charm. He's got good manners. Having doors thrown open for you and having your hand kissed mayn't be a good basis for matrimony, but it adds up on the credit side. He seemed to me attractive. And what's hardest of all to believe at this moment is that he didn't seem in the least overawed by my father. My father can be much more terrifying than the Comtesse, and most young men used to shake in their shoes, but Hubert didn't seem worried. So of course I thought that he was as brave as a lion. Now I know that it was simply because he didn't think my father could do him any harm.'

'But you weren't sure of him—or why the smuggling act?'

'My father's own habit of insuring a retreat. But now it's all over; it's done with, and I don't see why I should have my unfortunate love affair dragged out and hung up for everybody to examine. Why can't Hubert go away?'

'My own feeling is that he blames you, subconsciously, for the whole thing. If he hadn't met you and if you hadn't shown signs of falling for him, he probably wouldn't have taken a chance and proposed to you. You said you'd marry him, and the rest followed with what's known as the inevitability of fate. If you hadn't skipped off with the car, he'd at least have had something out of the wreck.'

'Well, the car's at the chateau, isn't it? As

Hubert pointed out to me, all that anybody has to do is take the keys off the peg in the kitchen when Léon isn't looking, hand them to Hubert and let him drive away.'

'He'd be picked up by the police.'

'You really think she'd put them on to him?'

'I'm certain of it. She doesn't like him and she doesn't feel the smallest sense of duty towards him.'

'You mean she'd actually let the poor fellow—'

'Now you've caught it,' said Sebastian.

'But he's come to appeal to Francine, and he'll hang round here waiting for her to do something for him, or think of something for him, or arrange something for him.'

'Yes. Unless we do it, or think of it, or arrange it. Any ideas?'

'Only to give him the car, and you've ruled that out.'

'What he really needs is a good steady job.'

'Who'd give him one?'

'Nobody.'

'So now what?'

He put out a hand and drew her to her feet.

'A drink,' he said. 'Do you know that it's Monsieur d'Arnaud's birthday tomorrow?'

'Yes, I know, but why the drink today?'

'Joss and I brought along some champagne for the dinner in his honour tomorrow, but I think it would be a good idea to get some more for tomorrow and to open a bottle now and

185

pour a little of it into Hubert.'

Jessica's eyebrows went up.

'As a reward for stealing his aunt's money?'

'As compensation for losing your father's.' Sebastian opened the front door with a flourish and lifted her hand to his lips. 'That's how you like it, isn't it?' he enquired.

Jessica made no reply. Hubert was coming down the stairs, and she waited for him; as she stood, Céline came out of the kitchen and rang the bell for lunch.

They gathered round the table, Maurice in his favourite place between Joss and Sebastian. All went well until the champagne was opened—and then Hubert, after one sip, put down his glass and burst into tears. Weeping, he looked round the circle of faces.

'You are so kind,' he said brokenly. 'You are being kind to me, and my aunt, who should be kind, does nothing.'

'Well, don't cry; drink up,' said Sebastian kindly.

'Why are you crying if we are kind?' asked Maurice in bewilderment.

Hubert accepted Joss's handkerchief, dried his tears and answered the question soberly.

'You are not my relations,' he explained, 'and so you need not have champagne for me. It is for my aunt to do this. But she, who should look after me, does not do so.'

'The Comtesse?'

'Yes. She has taken away my car.'

'But you could get it back,' suggested Maurice. 'She took away our table, but we took it back again.'

'That was not quite the same,' said Francine. 'If you have finished your fruit, Maurice, you need not remain at the table.'

Maurice left, but with less alacrity than usual. With a frowning backward glance at Hubert which showed genuine concern for his distress, he made his way to his grandfather's sitting room and looked round the door.

'I may come in, Grandpère?'

'Come in, of course,' said Monsieur d'Arnaud.

Maurice went in and sat cross-legged on the carpet at his grandfather's feet, and the old man looked down at him with a smile. The relationship between the two was one of great delicacy and restraint and—doubtless for these reasons—of great harmony. Maurice found his way several times a day to the little sitting room, but he did not stay long; a pleasant chat, a short exchange of news and no more; the two seemed to have an unspoken agreement on the matter. Each seemed to know that, agreeable though the company of the other was, it was a pleasure to be taken briefly and intermittently. They looked at one another with respect, with affection and perhaps with a little fear; their friendship was fragile and had to be handled gently.

'Hubert is sad,' began Maurice. 'His aunt

187

has taken away his car. You know Hubert?'

'I knew him when he was a young boy.'

'Was his aunt unkind to him when he was a young boy?'

'That is something that I do not know very much about,' said Monsieur d'Arnaud gently. 'Have you had a pleasant morning?'

'We found the kittens. The mother cat had hidden them away, but we found them. Henri's mother says that they are six weeks old. There are six kittens.'

'Will six people be found to take these six kittens which are six weeks old?'

'Henri's mother is going to ask. Can I have one, Grandpère?'

'But you are going back to Jersey, to your mother and father, in two weeks. You will not be able to take the kitten with you. The laws of Jersey do not permit it.'

'It is something called quarantine?'

'Yes. So perhaps it would be better if you did not have a kitten until you were again in Jersey. Did you visit Madame Seyboule?'

'No. She has locked her gate because all the boys walked too much upon the grass.'

'That was unwise; she has been very kind to you all, and if you anger her, see how much pleasure you lose. You must tell her that you are sorry.'

'We told her. She says that we must be sorry until the grass grows again. Tante Francine says that she will bake some things for her and I

188

will take them.'

'That is a very good idea.'

'And I saw Madame Jules,' said Maurice after a pause.

'Ah!' Monsieur d'Arnaud's voice changed subtly. The exclamation was soft and prolonged and had an undertone of tenderness. 'And what was she wearing?'

'She was wearing—' Maurice closed his eyes as an aid to memory—'a pink dress with—'

'Yes, I think that is a dress I know. With lace?'

'Yes, with lace. And with a big hat. So big. She sent you her compliments.'

Monsieur d'Arnaud put the tips of his fingers together and nodded with pleasure; eyes half-closed, he was picturing Madame Jules in her pink dress and shady hat. He smiled; how charming, how elegant she always looked. He would see her tomorrow, on his birthday; he would perhaps allow himself the pleasure of an extra visit to make up for the ones he had missed since his little accident in the waggon. The time had gone slowly; she had of course written, but that was not the same.

Madame Jules was his own age, and had spent her girlhood at Cloisy, within a stone's throw of the village. She was the widow of his greatest friend, Jules Kramer; she had been known upon her marriage as Madame Jules, to distinguish her from her mother-in-law, Madame Kramer. Old Madame Kramer was long since dead, but Madame Jules remained Madame Jules. On her husband's death, Monsieur d'Arnaud had written to Paris, where she had lived since her marriage; her old home, he told her, which had been sold, was now once more in the market; if she wished to buy it, he would arrange all the details for her.

The widow had come back to Cloisy, pale and drooping. The years had restored her health and her looks; they had also restored her spirits, which were lively. As her smiles increased, so, it was clear, did the admiration of Monsieur d'Arnaud. Always her friend, and her husband's, he saw her by degrees in another light; there had grown up between them a relationship as delicately balanced as that existing between himself and Maurice. Every evening before dinner in winter, after dinner in summer, he walked to the grey stone house—a toy chateau—in which she lived. He stayed perhaps an hour, drinking a little wine and listening to her chatter. Every Sunday she lunched at *Marielle*. There might be other meetings, other arrangements, but his evening visits and her weekly ones never varied. The whole village approved of the affair; the thin, elegant old widower, the pretty, well-dressed, smiling widow. Nobody seemed to expect more, or less: her wealth, it was thought, separated them, her wealth and his pride. The village understood perfectly.

Monsieur d'Arnaud's agreeable reverie was

brought to an end by the appearance of a figure in the open doorway. Looking up, he saw with astonishment that it was Hubert.

There was a moment's pause; many visitors found their way to the sitting room, but Hubert had never made one of the number and was not likely to be under the impression that he would be welcome.

But though Hubert stood hesitating on the threshold, he had a vague air of purpose. He had something to say, and in order to say it he had been prepared to risk something. He bad sailed in on the champagne and he was still feeling its support.

'Perhaps I disturb you, monsieur?' he asked humbly.

'Come in,' invited Monsieur d'Arnaud, and dismissed Maurice with a nod and a smile. 'Will you sit down?'

'I come only to pay my respects to you, monsieur. In the past, you were kind to me.'

'In the past, you were wiser, my dear Hubert,' said the old man drily. 'You had not given your aunt, or your friends, cause to close their doors. If you wish me to discuss the matter, I regret—'

'No, oh no, monsieur,' said Hubert hurriedly. 'It is not of my aunt that I have come to speak. What I have in mind concerns only Madame Jules.'

There was a pause.

'Madame Jules?' echoed the old man at last.

Hubert leaned forward and spoke eagerly.

'Madame Jules is a cousin, monsieur, of the Marquis de Moelle. He is the owner of the screen which my aunt was so anxious to buy.'

'I knew that the Marquis had sent a screen to the sale in Paris. I did not know then that your aunt had intended to buy it.'

'She was hoping very much to get it, monsieur. If she had told me why she was so anxious to buy it, perhaps I would not have acted so ... so hastily; I do not know. But she did not tell me that she wanted me to buy a screen in Paris while she herself bought a screen in London. This I only discovered by chance.'

'By what chance?'

'I spoke with Chevalier, of Lysaine. He brings from Salvan, from the trains, the furniture which my aunt buys. The screen from London has not yet come, but he has his instructions from my aunt, and from him—'

'You asked him what your aunt had bought, and he told you.'

'In a way, monsieur. I do not know what screen it was, but from my aunt's anxiety, I know that she wanted them to make a pair. And from this I know how I have disappointed her. She wanted a pair of screens, and through my stupidity she got only one. And now I wish to repair my mistake and to get her the screen which belongs to the Marquis de Moelle.'

'But the screen was sold in Paris. You yourself—'

'The screen was not sold, monsieur. I thought that you would know this. I thought that Madame Jules would have told you.'

'I have not seen Madame Jules since the day of the sale.'

'The screen was withdrawn, monsieur. The sale was not well attended because the strike was already beginning; buyers who were to come by train could not come. So for this, many things were withdrawn and among them, the screen of the Marquis de Moelle. And it came to me, monsieur, that if you could approach Madame Jules on my behalf, she would ask her cousin if he would allow me to arrange that my aunt should buy it. He is, as you know, monsieur, selling much of his property at La Rochelle; the screen will be offered for sale there. If I can say to my aunt that I have arranged that, through my efforts, the Marquis has consented to make terms with her for the purchase of the screen, she will perhaps forgive me for not having carried out her instructions. She is angry with me now. She wanted the screen very much, but she will of course learn that it was not sold. If then I can prove to her that I have ... that the screen ...'

He fell silent, his eyes fixed anxiously on the older man's face; his lips were trembling with suspense, or with the fear of a rejection.

'When I see Madame Jules tomorrow,' said Monsieur d'Arnaud quietly, 'I will tell her what you have said. I will not see her tonight;

193

my doctor has forbidden me to walk until tomorrow. I will tell her what you have said. More than that I will not do.'

Hubert rose to his feet in relief and began to utter stammered thanks; Monsieur d'Arnaud's upraised hand checked him. Bowing his farewells, he walked backwards out of the room and into the garden. There was no sign of Francine there or in the house; leaving a message of farewell with Céline, he went away.

Francine, with the others, had risen from the lunch table shortly after Hubert had left it. They had walked across the lane and now they were sitting on the grass in one of the clearings in the woods, talking of Hubert. Joss was saying little, and at last Francine looked across at him and spoke questioningly.

'You do not say very much; I think perhaps that you do not like Hubert? You think, perhaps, that he should not cry?'

Joss smiled at her.

'Frenchmen always cry,' he teased. 'They cry when they're happy and they cry, like Hubert, when they're miserable. Isn't that so?'

'Joss,' said Jessica, 'thinks we're all making too much fuss over Hubert. Don't you, Joss?'

'I think—' Joss hesitated and then went on more firmly. 'I think we're all being a little too sentimental. If we stopped lending him handkerchiefs and tried to find him a job of work, it might be more to the point. I don't want to sound too harsh, but he emerges—

doesn't he?—as a man who tried to marry a girl for her money, and stole some of his aunt's. If he were crying from remorse, I'd have nothing to say. But he isn't; he's crying because he didn't get what he was after.'

'You think,' asked Francine, 'that we should send him away?'

'No. That is, yes, but not without trying to do something for him. But so far, nobody has said anything to him about helping himself. He may look pathetic, but he's a man of twenty-five and that's too old, in my view, to cry just because he hasn't been successful in doing people down.'

'All right; so we try to be practical,' said Sebastian. 'We try to think of something that'll put him on his two feet. Well, he can't start out in business because he hasn't any capital and his aunt certainly won't give him any.'

'What he wants to do,' said Jessica, 'is to live at the chateau, not necessarily as its owner, but as a—well, a sort of caretaker. He loves the chateau. I think it's the only strong passion he'll ever have. And although I'm sorry he picked on me, I think his idea of marrying money and using it to lever himself into the chateau wasn't a bad idea. Isn't there any girl round here who'd like to swap a bankroll for life in a chateau?'

'I don't know one,' said Francine.

'Well, what have we got?' summed up Sebastian. 'He wants to live at the chateau and

195

is even prepared to go to the length of working for the Comtesse in order to be allowed to live there. But he's put himself in a position from which he can't hope to bargain. The only way he can get round his aunt now is by a bit of blackmail. Francine, is there anything in her past that wouldn't bear investigation?'

Francine shook her head a shade reluctantly.

'No. She is mean and selfish, but my father says that she has done nothing wicked.'

'It wouldn't have to be wicked; just indiscreet would do,' said Sebastian. 'Well, blackmail's out. Joss seems to have an idea. I can see it budding.'

'I was only wondering,' said Joss slowly, 'if there wasn't some way in which he could do his aunt a good turn.'

'Good turn?' echoed Sebastian. 'Where do you think that would get him?'

'You're not thinking he could soften her heart, are you?' asked Jessica.

'No. I wasn't thinking in terms of affection,' said Joss. 'He could only get at her from her vulnerable side—her business side. If he could put some money in her way, or some business in her way—'

'Or some furniture in her way. Furniture!' Sebastian brought out the word triumphantly. 'Furniture! If there was any way in which Hubert could get between her and a coveted bit of furniture—'

196

'How about the sale next week?' asked Joss.

'Let's all concentrate,' said Sebastian. 'There's a sale next week at La Rochelle, and the Comtesse will undoubtedly be at it. So we drive her there and she starts to bid. And what does she find? She finds Hubert there, outbidding her.'

There was a pause.

'Well, go on,' prompted Jessica at last. 'Hubert's there, outbidding her. Outbidding her with what? Money? Where's the money?'

'Why does it have to be money?' asked Sebastian. 'Why can't—'

'Bluff?' asked Joss. 'I don't think he'd have the nerve for it.'

'Why wouldn't he?' asked Jessica. 'He keeps his nerve well enough if he thinks things are going well. When he met me at St Malo, did he look nervous or anxious? Not a bit. He looked—'

'—possessive,' said Sebastian. 'If only we could get that look on his face when the bidding was reaching the sky—'

'Then what?' asked Francine. 'Suppose that the Comtesse will not bid higher?'

'We all know her. Do any of us here imagine for one moment,' said Sebastian, 'that she would drop out and let the despised Hubert buy something that she wanted? If it was a piece of furniture she really liked, she'd hang on to the end. If she didn't particularly like it, she'd hang on to spite Hubert.'

197

'And if Hubert hung on, too,' said Joss thoughtfully, 'then—'

'—then don't you see?' asked Sebastian. 'If he hung on, if he made her believe that he could outbid her, if it looked as though he could walk away with something that she wanted to get her claws into—Don't you see how that would change the relations between them? The seesaw would come down on her side and go up on his. He'd give her a devil of a fright, and she wouldn't despise him any more.'

'But if she dropped out of the bidding,' said Joss, 'that would leave Hubert in a fine old jam, wouldn't it?'

'The risk isn't worth considering,' said Sebastian. 'She'd never give way to Hubert. She'd hang on until she'd bid her last sou, thinking more and more of Hubert every moment. I think we should put the thing to Francine's father and ask whether he thinks it would work or not.'

'If his aunt sees Hubert at the sale,' said Joss, 'won't she call the police?'

'Not unless he'd got hold of the green car again,' said Sebastian.

Jessica, about to suggest disguising Hubert in the theatrical whiskers he had worn in the shrubbery of the chateau, changed her mind and remained silent. There was something in the discussion which had become earnest, if not serious. They were talking over the matter with a real desire to assist Hubert. Why this should be so, she was at a loss to decide; she herself, she realized, might have felt some sense of responsibility for what had befallen him, and Francine might regard him as an old friend who had never been given a chance to make something of himself, but to the two men he could only appear as a somewhat ridiculous figure whose troubles were no concern of theirs. A feeling of gratitude, strong but undefined, rose in her. It was nice of them, she told herself, to worry about him. This led her to conclude that they were both rather nice men, and she pondered the conclusion for some time. She had had her doubts about Sebastian, but there was no sign at this moment of his normally flippant and sometimes arrogant manner.

He looked up, and she met his eyes and smiled. It was a smile of apology for thinking less well of him than he merited, and she was unaware of how much warmth there was in the look.

'All right.' Sebastian rose. 'For the moment, we'll shelve it, but I think we've got on to something. It may have a faintly melodramatic flavour, but Monsieur d'Arnaud might tone it down a bit. Who wants a walk?'

The four walked through the woods in the direction of Lysaine; this time, Francine and Joss walked ahead and the other two followed.

'He's a nice man,' said Jessica thoughtfully, looking at Joss's tall form.

'Who? Joss? Of course,' agreed Sebastian. 'Do you know something? I've never, since I've known him, seen him so ... so sociable. He's shy; you can't get him to stay in the party as a general rule. You get him in, surround him with presentable girls and the next thing you know, he's well outside the circle, observing but not contributing. Here, there hasn't been any sign of his wanting to slide out and be on his own. And the reason is walking beside him now.'

'Francine?'

'Yes.'

'Does he like her?'

'He certainly wouldn't be here if he didn't. I might be the kind of man who'd take two meals a day off a girl I wasn't keen on, but not Joss. She's an easy girl to like.'

'Very easy. I've asked her to come and stay with me next time she comes to Jersey.'

'If you'll ask me at the same time, we can make up the foursome again.'

Jessica glanced up at him.

'Somehow,' she said thoughtfully, 'I've got the idea that Joss isn't the only one who's behaving uncharacteristically.'

'Me, too?'

'Yes. I'd say that you were more given to twosomes than to foursomes.'

'Two and two make four, don't they? I've tried more than once to interest Joss in girls; I've said, "I'll have this one and you have that

200

one and we'll all go somewhere or other", and then I've found that Joss has melted away. I don't mean that literally, of course; they weren't that kind of girl; but there I've been left with two women on my hands. And that's why we've come, gradually, to leave women out of our plans; we've gone off driving here and there and kept it strictly stag. And that's why this holiday is peculiarly good; Joss is, so to speak, still with us. That's why I'd like to repeat this at some other time in some other place. Do you often come to London?'

'About twice a year. You wouldn't get Joss and Francine to London, would you? Somehow I can't see either of them in a night club.'

'You wouldn't get Joss into one. Or if you did, he'd take one look at the cover charge and head for the door. And I think Francine would too; she's got a nice French thriftiness. I don't know much about her father's circumstances, but it's clear that Francine holds the purse strings.'

'She has to,' explained Jessica. 'Her father, she told me, is a spender, and there's not much to spend. So they've got an arrangement: he asks, and she tells him whether he can have it or not. He wants a car, but Francine says they can't afford one and I believe her.'

'I'd hate to see her in a car,' said Sebastian thoughtfully. 'Joss did a sketch of her—from memory. She was in the waggon and he'd splashed on the colour and it looked pretty effective.'

'We're going for a picnic in the waggon tomorrow,' said Jessica. 'To celebrate Monsieur d'Arnaud's birthday—only he isn't coming.'

'I gather there's a small but festive dinner party for him.'

'It's nothing really festive, Francine says. Just ourselves and somebody called Madame Jules.'

'Young and alluring?'

'Old but attractive, Francine says. She and Monsieur d'Arnaud are having a boy-and-girl romance. He's sweet,' said Jessica. 'I wouldn't mind having a romance with him myself. Don't you like those cunning little enigmatic glances he sends across the table?'

'Not particularly,' said Sebastian. 'But I like the old boy. He's the only man I ever met who made me feel that my hands were too big.'

'Hands? Or head?'

'Hands,' repeated Sebastian emphatically.

They came up to the others, who were sitting in a sunny patch, resting on a carpet of pine needles. Jessica dropped down beside Francine.

'This is the kind of exercise I like best,' she said. She leaned against a tree and closed her eyes. 'Lovely,' she murmured. 'Simply lovely.'

The others looked at her, at her slim, lovely legs, her limp, relaxed body and arched throat.

'Lovely. Simply lovely,' repeated Sebastian.

CHAPTER ELEVEN

Nobody knew what brought the Comtesse to the pink house on the following morning.

The waggon was before the gate, loaded with picnic baskets from which protruded bottles of wine. The horse, pawing the ground impatiently, stood still and seemed to stare in astonishment as the yellow car drove up the lane and halted before it; Léon, from the driving seat, stared back impassively. Maurice, seated in the waggon holding the reins, looked startled. Joss and Sebastian, in the garden, looked incredulous; only Francine, coming out of the front door with Maurice's mackintosh over her arm, gave no sign; the Comtesse might have been calling regularly every morning for years. She glanced at Joss and Sebastian, and they opened the gate and the car door and assisted the visitor to alight.

'Good morning,' said the Comtesse, with a nod of the head that included all present. 'I see that you are going to have a picnic. I should not have refused if you had invited me; it would have been a good return, I think, for the picnic which I gave to you the other day. Which is more, I would have brought the car and then you would not have had to go in that waggon

203

that fell into a ditch. I would not think it was safe to sit behind such a horse. Mademoiselle—' she turned to Francine—'I have come to enquire for your father after his accident.'

Nobody believed her for a moment; even the horse gave an incredulous snort. But the Comtesse was advancing up the path, and then the door of Monsieur d'Arnaud's sitting room opened and he came towards her with his slow, light, unhurried tread. She extended a hand and he bent courteously over it.

'It is pleasant out of doors,' he said. 'Shall we sit down?'

The pronoun, it became clear, included not only himself and the Comtesse; he was placing seats for Francine and for Jessica, who came into the garden and stopped short upon seeing the Comtesse. He sent a brief look towards Joss and Sebastian, and there was something in it that told them that they, too, were to be members of the group seated round the Comtesse.

There was a pause during which everybody wondered whether the news of Hubert's visit had reached his aunt. Though she seldom came to Cloisy, she was not above shopping there occasionally in order to glean items of information concerning the local inhabitants. Hubert, moreover, had exercised little discretion during his visit; fortified by the champagne and the friendliness of all at

Marielle, he had taken a walk round the village and greeted several boyhood acquaintances.

The Comtesse, however, began to speak only of general matters. It became obvious, from her growing impatience, her hints and her angry glances at Monsieur d'Arnaud, that she had intended to see him alone, but he showed no sign of understanding what she wanted; he had held forth on the weather, the price of food and was about to launch into some statistics regarding the harvest when the Comtesse broke into his sentence.

'These young ones—are they not going away on their picnic?' she asked in exasperation. 'Look at the little boy in the waggon—the horse will become impatient and he will be carried off.'

'There is no hurry,' said Monsieur d'Arnaud tranquilly. 'There is the whole day.'

'But for me, no; for me there is not the whole day,' said the Comtesse, losing patience. 'I have come to say something to you, monsieur, and I would like to say it to you only.'

Monsieur d'Arnaud raised his shoulders in a deeply regretful shrug. Joss thought that he had never before realized how many things could be said, how much expressed by a shrug. Monsieur d'Arnaud said far more with his shoulders than with his tongue.

'Ah, Comtesse,' he said. 'If I had known.' He took a watch from his pocket and looked at it. 'The time ... already, I regret, I am late for a rendezvous.'

There was nothing for the Comtesse to do but rise. She did so with ill-concealed anger and the barest of farewells, and Sebastian escorted her to her car.

'I do not think that this is grateful,' she told him, 'that you come here every day and stay all day. You owe me something, is it not? First you promise to drive me, but when I look for you to ask you, where are you? You are here in this house. They cannot want you all this time; it is not polite, I think, to throw yourselves on to strangers.'

Sebastian made no audible reply. They had reached the car and he was holding the door open. The Comtesse hesitated and then spoke in a different tone.

'There is a sale at La Rochelle next week. I would like you or your friend to drive me.'

'We'll both go along,' said Sebastian.

'You do not know—' the Comtesse glanced over her shoulder and lowered her voice—'you have not heard if any others are going?'

'No, I haven't,' said Sebastian.

'I came here to—well, it does not matter. It does not make any difference. He is too clever, that old d'Arnaud, to give away what he knows.'

She got into the car and Léon drove her away and the drive to the picnic, so disagreeably delayed, went forward swiftly. Sebastian took the reins; Maurice was on one

206

side of him and Francine on the other; behind were Jessica and Joss. Céline waved from the doorway; Madame Seyboule waved from her window; Monsieur d'Arnaud stood at the gate and bowed and smiled; they might have been going away for a month.

When they had gone, Monsieur d'Arnaud turned and went into the house and presently emerged, groomed and elegant, and made his way to the grey stone house. A smile was on his lips; it was his birthday, and in the evening, when the young people returned from the picnic, there would be a small dinner in his honour. But for the moment, he was alone and on his way to enjoy an even greater pleasure: lunch with his old friend, Madame Jules. He went with all the more eagerness since this was his first visit to her since his accident on the way back from Salvan; she had sent him frequent amusing little notes, but that was a poor substitute for the pleasure of watching her as she talked.

A maid admitted him and led him to the green-and-white drawing room; in a few moments Madame Jules came in, and for a time Monsieur d'Arnaud could do nothing but gaze at her in quiet appreciation. She looked, as usual, charming; once again he was to tell himself that age could be as attractive as youth. He could not have said what it was about her that gave the impression of undying youthfulness; she dressed well, but her clothes were entirely suitable to her age. It was, he thought, something to do with her easy, gentle, graceful femininity; age could not take away her humour or her quick sympathy or her gay spirit.

She had given him one hand; the other held a small package.

'I am glad that you could come this morning, Emile,' she said. 'I said to myself, "In some ways, perhaps, he is a very stupid man, but he will not wait until the evening to come and allow his old friend to greet him." A happy birthday! Are you feeling better? I would have come to see you, but you know that my cousin and his wife have been here? I could not go without them, and three of us would have been too much. I wish that we could speak on the telephone, for then we could have such long talks! But you would only say yes, no, yes, no—it would be so dull! Now I shall give you this little parcel and you must open it and look inside and see what a kind friend you have in me.'

There was a tiepin inside, long and slender, with a single tiny jewel, ideally suited to its purpose, which was that of securing Monsieur d'Arnaud's snowy cravat. She pinned it on for him and stood surveying him, her head on one side.

'It is perfect,' she pronounced. 'I should not say so, but it is perfect. Now you may say so, too.'

'It is perfect, and you are the kindest woman in the world, but I owe you too much to attempt to put any of it into words.'

'Good. Then let us sit and talk of other things. You must have so much to tell me. I have seen little Maurice. Is he to be with you for long?'

'Not on this visit; he must return in less than two weeks because he and his mother must buy new clothes before school begins. He has grown out of everything.'

'You have visitors besides Maurice? My maid told me. If we had no maids, how should we get our news? You said nothing of this when you answered my little notes. Tell me about the visitors.'

'Later. There was a visitor this morning, and you will not guess who it was.'

'Tell me.'

'It was the Comtesse.'

He was pleased with the effect of his announcement; one did not often see Madame Jules sitting in stunned silence.

'No!' she exclaimed at last. 'You are joking. No, you are not joking, because a visit from her would not be a joke. What did she want?'

'That was the first thing I asked myself. But I did not find out what she wanted, because I decided that I would not give her the opportunity to tell me. I imagine that it was something about Hubert.'

'Hubert? Why, after all these years,' asked

Madame Jules wonderingly, 'would the Comtesse pay her first visit to your house in order to talk about Hubert?'

'Because Hubert seems to have become, surprisingly, the centre of everybody's attention. Before he came in person to visit us, others had come to remind us of him. First it was a young girl from Jersey; next, two Englishmen. The garden has looked to me very overcrowded.'

'All this has been going on and nobody has come to tell me about it?' asked Madame Jules indignantly. 'If I had known that you had kept all this news from me, I would not have given you that beautiful pin. Who are these people? When did they come? Why did they come?'

'You are interested in all this?'

'Oh, don't be so infuriating! Talk, talk, talk!'

'Very well. I shall tell you the story clearly. Everything begins with the screen that your cousin sent to the sale in Paris.'

'De Moelle?'

'Yes. He told you, I suppose, that it had been withdrawn?'

'Yes. He told me something else, too, but that can wait until I have heard this story. Go on.'

'The Comtesse gave Hubert money to go to the sale in Paris and bid for the screen.'

'Then she is losing her wits,' said Madame Jules promptly, 'or you have got the facts upside down. She would never trust anybody

210

with money, and she would never dream of trusting Hubert with anything.'

'But she did. She sent him to the sale in Paris because she herself had to go to an equally important sale in London. So she—What is the matter?'

For the second time that morning, Madame Jules was regarding him openmouthed. He waited for her to speak, but she seemed to find difficulty in enunciating.

'The Comtesse ... went to London?' she brought out at last.

'Yes. What is so extraordinary about that?'

'It is—' Madame Jules stopped and shook her head. 'No. You must tell me your story first, and then I think that we shall know why the Comtesse went to see you this morning. Go on about Hubert.'

'He did not go to the sale. With the money, he bought an expensive car. When the Comtesse heard that he had not been at the sale, she left London at once; she was convinced that if he had found the courage to rob her of her money, he would come to the chateau, believing her to be still in London, and steal some of her furniture. But when she landed at St Malo, the strike had begun; she bought a broken-down sort of taxi and later, if you will believe it, another hack of a disagreeable yellow colour, and she brought the two Englishmen back as chauffeurs.'

'But wait a moment,' said Madame Jules.

'Hubert could not have done this alone. He is a coward and he is also a fool. He must have had accomplices.'

'He acted alone. He had planned to marry the girl from Jersey; she is rich, and the car was bought to impress her. At least, that is what she thinks, but I feel myself that with money in his hands for the first time, he was only buying something for which he had longed all his life.'

'He bought a car and married the girl?'

'No. He gave himself away at St Malo, so she drove away in the car and came to the chateau because one of her suitcases had been put by mistake into the Comtesse's car.'

Madame Jules stared at him.

'This is all very confused, Emile. If you were Jules, I would accuse you of having drunk the champagne before the feast. If all this has been going on at the chateau, what is it to do with you?'

'One of the Englishmen came from Jersey, and was asked to look after Maurice. They brought him in the car, but Francine and I, as you know, were delayed. They got into the house and the Comtesse took away a table.'

'But this is absurd!'

'Yes.'

'The accident hasn't deranged you?'

'Perhaps. But I am trying to tell you the facts.'

'Facts? Facts? The Comtesse, who is the meanest woman on earth, gives Hubert, whom

212

she detests, a large sum of money, and takes away a table, and the suitcase is mixed up, the marriage is off and—Emile, you have a fever.'

Monsieur d'Arnaud, after some time, succeeded in disentangling for her all the details; Madame Jules then said that it was she and not he who had the fever.

'It is fantastic!' she said. 'And what is most fantastic of all is that you do not yet know why the Comtesse called on you this morning.'

'You think that you know?' he enquired mildly.

'You shall hear. You know, of course, that De Moelle is selling his house, and everything that is in it, at La Rochelle. It is sad; it is a tragedy, but there is no longer money for two establishments, and I think that he is wise to keep the Paris house and let the one at La Rochelle go. But that is beside the point. The point is only the screens.'

'The screen.'

'The screens, Emile. There are two, as you should know.'

'Two screens?' said Monsieur d'Arnaud slowly.

'A pair of screens. You may have forgotten, Emile, but you certainly knew the story. The screens were a pair, but one of them was lost in the Revolution. Surely you—'

'You know, my dear—' Monsieur d'Arnaud's voice was, for him, almost brisk— 'this has suddenly become extraordinarily interesting.'

'Of course. You knew that the Comtesse must have had a very strong reason for going to see you; it was not for love. It was because she found out—how, I cannot tell you—that on the day my cousin was to sell his screen in Paris, a similar one was offered for sale in London; she went to London and bought it and then found that Hubert had not bought the one in Paris; knowing, now, that it is to be offered for sale at La Rochelle, she wishes to find out from you whether my cousin knows that the screens are a pair. She may even wish to persuade you to persuade me to persuade him to sell the second one to her privately.'

'Hubert came to me yesterday,' said Monsieur d'Arnaud, 'and asked me that. He wanted you to use your influence with your cousin.'

'He does not know that the screens are a pair?'

'He does not know that they are the pair you speak of. Why does De Moelle not—'

'Keep the second one? Because rather than part with hers, the Comtesse would have it buried with her. She does not like any of us, Emile. If I thought she would sell it, I would make her an offer, but I know that she would refuse. Poor Hubert, it is a pity that he offended her so hopelessly; he—What are you laughing at?'

'At you. At those young people yesterday.

214

At Francine. They all knew that he had robbed his aunt and almost married a young girl for her money, and what did they say? They said, "Poor Hubert."'

'If you had to take sides,' demanded Madame Jules, 'on whose side would you be? On the Comtesse's, or on Hubert's?'

'My sympathies would perhaps be with Hubert, but—'

'You need not go on. You want to say that the Comtesse is the injured one? Perhaps. But she is also the one we like even less than we like Hubert.'

'That is a woman's argument. I think that Hubert is a worthless young man and I think that they had all much better leave him to himself instead of making up plots to rehabilitate him.'

'Plots?'

'They were speaking to me about it at dinner last night—the girl from Jersey and the two Englishmen and also, you will be surprised to hear, Francine. They asked my advice, but I did not give it. They had strong sympathies but weak suggestions. They had much better leave Hubert to work things out for himself.'

'Usually,' said Madame Jules judiciously, 'you are a very sensible man. Today—it is the champagne, I think—you are not so wise. If you did not encourage those young people to help Hubert, you were wrong, because they see something which you do not; namely, that

215

Hubert is quite incapable of working things out for himself. If he had had advantages, if he had in all his life had somebody, anybody, any one person who had given him a word of good advice or had made an attempt to guide him, to train him, then he might have been equipped, as any other man, to make his own way. But think for yourself; put your mind back and try to remember. You know what his life has been. If you discouraged those young people from helping him, you were very wicked.'

'I said nothing.'

'You can say nothing very discouragingly.'

'I told you that their plans were weak.'

'What plans did they have?'

'They arrived at the conclusion that if Hubert could prevent his aunt, in some way, from getting something she really wanted, she would respect him, or bargain with him, or forgive him, I don't know which.'

'Something she wants? But all she wants in this world is furniture.'

'Yes. So much they understood. They thought that he should go to the sale at La Rochelle and bid against her for the things she wanted there, and as I told them that she wanted the screen, they decided that that would be the thing. There was only one flaw in the arrangement: he had no money to bid with.'

'They meant that he should pretend to be buying the screen?'

'Yes. You can see—'

'Was he to pretend he was buying for himself, or for somebody else?'

'What difference does that make, my dear? The Comtesse would not be taken in for a moment.'

'That is true.' Madame Jules frowned. 'But you know, Emile, the idea was not such a bad one.'

'To pit Hubert against his aunt?'

'Yes. If she imagined that he was serious, that he had in some way discovered what she herself knew—that the screen was the second of the pair—then I think that she would be alarmed. I think that she would do anything, bid anything to get the screen for herself.'

'That is all very well, but you are leaving out a very important point.'

'No, I am not. You are going to say that he cannot bid because he has no money. That is true. He could not bid for himself. But he could bid for somebody else.'

Monsieur d'Arnaud stared at her, and for once it was a look of noncomprehension. The maid came in to announce lunch, and he rose absently and gave his arm to Madame Jules. They had taken their places at the table and were unfolding their napkins before he gave up the problem with a shrug.

'I do not understand,' he said. 'For whom is he to bid?'

Madame Jules looked at him across the table

and gave him an enchanting smile.

'For me, my poor tortoise-brain,' she said. 'For me.'

CHAPTER TWELVE

Dinner that evening was a candlelit feast for six. At the beginning of the meal, conversation was general, but one by one the others fell silent and Madame Jules was left, to her obvious satisfaction, alone on the stage.

Monsieur d'Arnaud was silent not so much from habit as from sheer enjoyment; the food was light but excellent, the company congenial and Madame Jules in her gayest mood. In his opinion—and he did not think it in any way influenced by the champagne—she was as lovely and as fresh as the two young girls. The two young girls, while not going as far as this, thought her extremely amusing, and Jessica, studying her across the table, hoped that she would wear as well as this attractive Frenchwoman. Joss and Sebastian liked her stories, which had a faintly racy flavour, and encouraged her to talk.

There had been for a time a suggestion, or a threat, that Hubert would be present; he had telephoned to Francine during the afternoon and told her frankly that he would come if he were asked; Monsieur d'Arnaud, however, had firmly declined to have him. Dinner was his favourite meal and he would not on any evening have wished to have it spoilt; on his birthday it was even less to be thought of. Hubert's name, however, was brought up by Madame Jules halfway through the meal, and she laid her plan before them all and then sat smiling happily at its effect on all save Monsieur d'Arnaud, who knew it already.

'You mean, Madame—' Sebastian leaned forward and spoke incredulously—'you mean that you're going to give Hubert instructions—'

'—to outbid his aunt, no matter how much she may pay,' said Madame Jules. 'Yes, I mean that. Monsieur d'Arnaud told me this morning that you had been speaking of Hubert and wondering what could be done; you had realized that his only wish was to go back to the chateau and live there with his aunt—why he should wish this, only God knows, for He knows all. You would have said that an aunt like that would be one to be lived as far away from as possible, but it is Hubert's life, is it not? And you were right in saying that he could have no possible hope of approaching her except by this one path. This is her only weakness. She has many failings, but she has only one weakness, I think.'

'I pity her,' said Francine.

'Then you are a good girl.' Madame Jules laid her fingers, heavy with beautiful rings, upon the girl's for a moment. 'You have a good heart. But I am a flint-hearted old woman and I have no love for the Comtesse, and no pity. She could, even now, lead a pleasant life, but she prefers to lead a lonely and a selfish one. Hubert, as all of us here know, is not much of a man, but he is her only living relative—of any nearness—and he could be useful to her. I wonder she does not see that.'

'But why should you do this for Hubert?' asked Joss.

'For Hubert?' Madame Jules leaned back in her chair and gave a sound between a gurgle and a giggle; it was so infectious that the others laughed with her. 'For Hubert? Oh, no, no, no, my dear Joos, I am not doing this for Hubert. That is a very droll idea! And it occurs to me that Joos—this is a very droll name. Why are you called this?'

'Joss. I was christened James Joseph,' said Joss, 'and somehow the James was dropped and Joseph became Joss. These things happen.'

'Well, my dear James, or Joseph, or Joss, you must not for one instant run away with the idea that I am a kind old woman who is helping poor Hubert. No, no, no. I am a vindictive old woman who is using this good, this irresistible opportunity to pay off an old score against the Comtesse.'

She paused with pretty expectancy and Sebastian smiled at her.

'We're waiting,' he said.

'Shall I tell them, Emile?' she asked.

'Nothing is going to prevent you, my dear.'

'Very well. It was a long time ago,' began Madame Jules, 'but it was something that one doesn't forget.'

'Especially,' put in Monsieur d'Arnaud gently, 'when one doesn't wish to.'

'Well, let them judge. It was after the death of the Comte,' said Madame Jules. 'The Comtesse had already turned the chateau into a warehouse, and she was to be seen at every important sale; sometimes I used to go myself, and we met but did not speak; like Francine and her father, I am a Protestant, and she does not love us. On one occasion at a sale, there was something that I wanted very much; it was a table at which, it is believed, Madame de Pompadour played at cards with the King. A beautiful table. I wanted it very much, and I went to the sale determined to buy it if possible. And the Comtesse went to the sale with exactly the same idea. She knew that I was going to be a serious and certainly a very expensive rival; she could hope to outbid the dealers, but she knew that I would go on. So what did she do?'

'If you wait,' murmured Monsieur d'Arnaud, 'Madame Jules will tell you.'

'Everybody was walking about slowly,' said Madame Jules, 'waiting for the second part of the sale to begin. I found myself near the Comtesse; she was in front of me. She opened the door of a room and looked inside; I,

221

supposing that there was something of interest in there, went inside. The room was empty. When I turned to go out again, I found that the Comtesse had gone away—and she had locked the door behind her. I was,' she declared with fine dramatic effect, 'a prisoner.'

'You hammered frenziedly upon the door,' prompted Monsieur d'Arnaud, 'and—'

'Emile, please; I tell this story very well; far better than you. I made a great noise in that room, I can tell you,' she resumed. 'People came, but they could not find the key; she had thrown it on the floor in a corner and they could not see it. They did everything that was stupid and nothing that was sensible; they rattled the door and said that it must be stuck and not locked—who would lock it? They did not send a message to delay the sale for a few moments; they did not look properly for the key. So when the key was found, the table was lost. The Comtesse had got it; it was hers. Is this something to forget? One's religion says yes, one's instinct says no. But I never for one moment thought of returning the blow. It was only this morning, when I heard of your plan to help Hubert, that the picture came to me: the sale, the Comtesse bidding for something that she wants very much, for—'

'Why?' asked Joss.

Madame Jules looked like someone who, having hurried past an object, returns in order to examine it more carefully.

'What did you say?' she asked.

'Why does the Comtesse want the screen so much?'

'If you had waited,' said Madame Jules reproachfully, 'I would have come to that. The reason that she wants the screen so much is because she has discovered something that scarcely anybody else knows, something that even my cousin, who owns one of the screens, did not know at that time: that the screen at the sale in London was the twin to the one being offered by my cousin in Paris. Both screens, originally, were in the De Moelle palace in Paris, which was burned down during the Revolution. One screen was saved, the other lost. My cousin's family did not succeed in finding out anything about it except that it had been carried out of the palace. The Comtesse knew the story, and she must have found out that two unusual but very similar screens were being offered for sale on the same day; the fact that she trusted Hubert with so large a sum of money proves that there was something very special calling her to London. And now she has one of the screens and my cousin has the other. He cannot afford to buy hers, even if she would sell it. I would make her an offer, but I think you will find that your plan will produce a very good price for my cousin. Hubert does not yet know that the screens are a true pair. I will tell him, and he will understand that the Comtesse will go to almost any lengths to buy the second one. I shall tell him that there is no limit to the price I am prepared to pay. And as he has shown that, where his own interests are concerned, he can sometimes act to his own advantage, he will understand that this is his chance to bargain with his aunt.'

'You're not going to tell him why you're doing this?' asked Sebastian.

'But no! He will be sure that I am anxious to keep one of the screens in the family. He will not know, but the Comtesse will. She will be quite sure that I want my revenge; being a woman, she will know how much a woman will pay to get it.'

'Will you go to the sale?' asked Joss.

'Yes. I shall go because Hubert, if the bidding goes too high, may lose his courage. I shall be there to give him confidence. If the Comtesse retires, the screen will be mine and I shall give it to De Moelle and his wife with my love—but I do not think the Comtesse will retire. I think that she will do as you say: she will come to terms with Hubert.'

'But if Hubert is to bargain with her,' said Joss, 'and if he is to use the screen as a weapon, he can only get into her favour by allowing her to buy the screen. Which means that he stops bidding. Which means that he disregards your instructions.'

'Which means that he betrays my trust,' said Madame Jules, and smiled slowly. 'But my dear Joss,' she asked, 'what else did you expect, what else does anyone expect of poor Hubert?'

*   *   *

'And you must admit,' said Jessica reflectively to Sebastian, half an hour later, 'that there's something about Frenchwomen.'

They were walking slowly up the lane; Jessica was a little uncertain how she had got there, but Sebastian knew. The candlelight, the dinner and perhaps the champagne had gone to his head; he had enjoyed himself very much, and a stroll in the darkness with a lovely girl was the way to add the last touch of felicity.

'Yes, there's something about Frenchwomen,' he agreed. 'That is, about attractive ones like Madame Jules. But when it comes to women and beauty, does nationality really come into it?'

'Why ask me? If we've got on to women and beauty, you're the expert,' said Jessica.

'I don't like that "expert."'

'Well, connoisseur, then; do you like connoisseur any better?'

'A little,' said Sebastian, testing it. 'Connoisseur. It all depends how you'd define it.'

'It's someone who knows all about his subject.'

'Then it doesn't apply.'

'No?'

'No. I like women—who doesn't? I'm thirty-four,' said Sebastian, 'and I suppose I've been around and I suppose I'm more of an experimenter than Joss. But he's one of the lucky ones; he can be exposed to a lot of danger without getting harmed. He's steady, stable, if you like. He keeps his head.'

'You lose your head?'

'No. But I want more of certain things than he seems to do. He's with Francine now, in a moonlit garden on a warm night; the only people in view are Francine's father and Madame Jules, and they're sitting on the terrace talking about the old days and not worrying about what any of the rest of us are doing. But Joss ... what'll Joss talk about?'

'You.'

'Well, there it is in a nutshell. You and he were off on your own for a long time at the picnic this morning. What did he talk about?'

'You.'

'It's a big subject,' admitted Sebastian, 'but not as big as that. Why didn't you get him off it?'

'Why? It's very revealing.'

'What makes you think I want to be revealed? If I appear as a woman's man, I'm being misrepresented. I like women's society—if I like the women, that is. What's more, when I'm in their society in circumstances like these, a feeling of gratitude—or something—comes over me and I express it. Anything wrong in that?'

'Nothing. You're not thinking of expressing it now, are you?'

'To be honest,' said Sebastian with some surprise, 'the idea wasn't in my mind. I daresay it's creeping nearer, but at this moment my gratitude embraces more than one woman; it embraces three. Four, counting the Comtesse.'

'The Comtesse?'

'I suppose it sounds odd. But I'm grateful to her for touching off the whole thing. For bringing us here. I'm grateful to Francine for letting us come to *Marielle*. I'm grateful to you for suggesting it. I'm grateful to Madame Jules for coming up to scratch in the Hubert situation. This may be an odd holiday from some points of view, but I've enjoyed myself—I am enjoying myself—more than I've done in my life.'

'So's Joss.'

'Did he say so?'

'Yes. Not in a long speech, like you; he merely stated it briefly.'

'Don't get the idea that he's inarticulate. When he gets angry, for instance, he can talk to some purpose.'

'I know that. Didn't my father tell me?'

'He's at his best when there aren't any women around. They dry him up, somehow.'

'He didn't dry up this morning.'

'You underrate yourself. Moreover, there's a lot about you that's like Francine. I didn't think so when I first met you, but I do now.

You've been kind to Joss, and I'm damn grateful. It takes a nice woman to see how nice he is. I only hope Francine will see it.'

There was a pause.

'She has seen it,' said Jessica.

'You mean ... she likes him?'

'Very much. Why? Are you trying to throw them together?' asked Jessica.

'I'm ... I don't know. I only know that for years I've tried to find the perfect wife for Joss—a sort of very special wife. And when you come to think of it, who could be more perfect than Francine?'

'Who indeed?'

'You're not laughing, are you?'

'No, I'm listening. Go on.'

'Well, look. She's lovely, but she's much more. She's a good manager; she won't throw Joss's money about, which is a good thing because he hasn't got much. She's a magnificent cook; she'll run his house like a dream. If he doesn't get far with her here, he can pick it up next time she comes to Jersey. When you come to think of it, they're the ideal couple: they're both rather shy, they're both quiet, they're both steady. The more you look at it, the more inevitable it appears. They're as much alike as ... as you and I are.'

'I'm not in the least like you,' said Jessica. 'I wouldn't care if I never saw a beautiful woman again.'

'What you're suffering from,' said

228

Sebastian, 'is reaction.'

'What am I having a reaction from?'

'From men. From marriage. I don't blame you. For the moment, you've had enough. And that's why I haven't got my arms round you now. That's why I'm not taking advantage of the wonderful night—and the wonderful opportunity. And the wonderful girl. If I kissed you now, you wouldn't—well, you wouldn't cooperate, would you?'

'No. I wouldn't,' said Jessica.

'That's what I mean. We've got to let that Hubert affair settle. For the moment, you've had enough, as I said, and although it seems a terrible waste of opportunity, I'm not going to kiss you because I have a feeling you don't want me to. Am I right?'

'Quite right. You know something, Sebastian?' said Jessica slowly. 'You're a very nice person.'

Sebastian smiled down at her in the darkness.

'How can you know that—yet?' he asked.

'Joss told me,' said Jessica.

CHAPTER THIRTEEN

'And the thing to do, as I told you before,' said Sebastian to Joss a week later, 'is not to talk about *me* but about *her*.'

They were walking back to the chateau after dinner, as they had done each night after spending the day in the company of Jessica and Francine. Sebastian's voice held the despair of a teacher who, having laboured long over a backward pupil, begins to feel that the time has been wasted. He had devoted himself to the pleasant task of uniting Joss and Francine; he had appointed himself godfather to the scheme; he had talked without stopping every night from Francine's gate to the door of the chateau and every word had been, he felt, a pearl of wisdom taken from the riches of his own experience.

He had worked, as far as he could see, to no purpose. His daily efforts to split up the party of four into two pairs had met with no result; his nightly advice to Joss on their way home had been received with attention and gratitude but had failed to produce the smallest spark of initiative in the recipient.

'You don't seem to get the idea at all,' continued Sebastian. 'When you're with a girl, she wants to talk about you—or about herself. The last thing she wants to hear is the history of a man who isn't present and who would be very much in the way if he were.'

'But people know all about themselves,' demurred Joss. 'What they want to hear about is other people.'

'That's where you're wrong,' said Sebastian. 'When it comes to conversation between the

230

sexes, it's a case of *plus ca change, plus c'est la même chose*. If this holiday hasn't done anything else, it's polished up our French.'

'But I don't like talking about myself.'

'It comes naturally, when you're in love, and anybody with a vestige of intelligence can see that you're in love.'

'Me?'

'You. Let me prove it to you. Aren't you more silent than you ever were?'

'I hadn't noticed.'

'Well, I have. When we're having breakfast at the chateau, I talk to you and you don't even listen.'

'I do when you come out with anything worth listening to.'

'That isn't all. You moon.'

'I what?'

'You go about mooning. You moon all the time. You brood. If you remember, the very first night we walked home like this after being at *Marielle*, I issued a general warning; I said that if we didn't look out, we'd fall in love. Both of us. And that's exactly what's happened.'

'How can you tell?'

'To be absolutely honest with you,' said Sebastian, 'I saw the symptoms in you first, and then I looked for them in myself, and caught myself doing things I'd never done before. I found myself thinking of the most extraordinary things.'

231

'Such as?'

'Such as whether it was time I put my son's name down for Harrow. Observe that I haven't yet got a son.'

'What else?'

'I've gone off my food.'

'Gone off? But at lunch today, I saw you—'

'I didn't mean Francine's food. I meant yours. Breakfast. Remember what whacking breakfasts I used to put away? Now what do I eat? Practically nothing. Couple of eggs, a few slices of bacon and a few bits of toast.'

'Well, I wouldn't call that—'

'But the thing that made me understand, at last, that I was in love—really in love—was the fact that I felt damn miserable. I get up feeling miserable; I feel miserable all through breakfast; then we go to *Marielle* and with every step we take, I feel better. I feel fine all day and then I feel miserable again when I leave.'

'Me, too,' confessed Joss.

'And that's the proof,' summed up Sebastian.

'What is? Feeling damn despondent?'

'Yes. Always, before, when I've fancied myself in love, I've felt wonderful. Exhilarated. Now, when it's the real thing, I'm down in the depths.'

'But—'

'Which in itself is clear proof. Take Shakespeare. He knew all there was to know

232

about lovers, and what does he say about them? How does he describe them? Happy as sandboys? No. "Sighing like furnace" was how he put it, and that's how an outsider, a detached observer, would describe us. We're in love, Joss, and all that remains now is to find out how we stand with Jessica and Francine.'

'But—'

'Well, we can leave Jessica out for the moment; I'm not going to hurry her. You'll have to be careful not to rush Francine too much, too; she's a gentle little thing and you'll have to work up to it gradually.'

'Work up to what?'

'To your proposal, of course! For heaven's sake, do you or do you not want to get married?'

'Yes, I do. I do very much. But—'

'Very well, then. You've got to find the right words, and when you've found them, you've got to say them in the right way.'

'But how on earth can I think up a—'

'In a matter of this kind,' said Sebastian, 'a man's on his own. I've done what I can for you, but after this it's up to you.'

'That's all very well,' said Joss, 'but I can't—'

'All you have to do is prepare a simple little speech and get it off to Francine—and soon. The weather's been kind so far, but it's bound to break soon, and we won't be able to wander about as we've been doing. We'll be indoors

233

and you won't be able to get her on her own. So think out what you want to say to her, and say it as soon as possible.'

'Yes, but—'

'Look at it this way. You and I, you'll admit, have waited a long time to find the right girls—and here they are. Agreed?'

'Yes, agreed.'

'Very well, then. Don't let's waste any more time. I want a settled home and I want children and so, I imagine, do you.'

'Yes, but—'

'But what?'

'Isn't it ... too soon? We've hardly known them—'

'The trouble with people like you,' said Sebastian, 'is that they read too much lurid fiction. We all know how it goes inside the paper covers: they meet, they love, they'd like to marry, they can't marry. For the next thirty-two chapters they fight the obstacles. On page seven hundred they despair of marrying. On page eight hundred it's clear that they've got to marry, and fast. On page one thousand they're married. Why don't you forget fiction and face facts? The facts are that the four of us—you and I, Francine and Jessica—have had an absolutely unique chance of getting to know one another well. We could have known each other for years, meeting occasionally, without getting to the stage we've got to here in Cloisy. And now, if we've got any sense, we'll try to put the thing on to a permanent basis—and if the girls like us, there aren't any obstacles that I can see and so we don't have to wait until page one thousand just to torture the readers. So think it over tonight. Decide what you want to say. Tomorrow, say it. If I could help you, I would, but at a time like this, you've got to act for yourself. Any questions?'

'Well ... no. Except—'

'Except what?'

'Nothing,' said Joss.

*　　*　　*

If the weather was breaking, the next morning gave no sign of it. Sebastian, eating his eggs and bacon and toast, saw with satisfaction that the sun was shining warmly. Even the entrance of the Comtesse could not detract from the brightness of the day.

She sat down with her customary calm expectation of being fed, but they heard less, this morning, of the grating voice. Joss, putting her plate before her, saw that she was moody and depressed and wondered for a whimsical moment whether she, too, was in love.

'You are going, of course,' she said, 'to those people?'

'To *Marielle*? Yes. At least, we're going on a picnic,' said Sebastian.

'They are not hospitable for nothing,' said the Comtesse. 'They entertain you because you are men, and where there is a young girl to be married, young men are, naturally, encouraged to come. But see how I overcame my prejudices and went to see them. What came of it? Nothing. Did they invite me when there was old d'Arnaud's birthday? No. It is the work of that woman who calls herself Madame Jules. She calls herself that because she thinks that people will mistake her for a young woman. If old d'Arnaud were not under her influence, one could have asked him some things about the sale tomorrow, but if he knows anything, he will not say it. He is a sour old man. You will not gain much, I can tell you, from knowing such people.'

This prophecy did not discourage Joss and Sebastian from setting out immediately after breakfast and going briskly in the direction of *Marielle*. As they drew near, their steps became slower and silence fell; Sebastian, glancing once or twice at Joss, saw that his brows were drawn in a heavy frown; he had the air of a man wrestling with a problem, and Sebastian did not disturb him.

Once at the house, however, there was not time for brooding; the horse had to be caught and harnessed; rugs and hampers had to be carried out. Maurice's mackintosh was brought out and then taken in again; with the sudden realization that the end of his visit was near, he had elected to spend as much of the remaining time as possible with his

236

companions.

The others set out, but there was not, today, as much talking as usual; the two men seemed to be lost in thought. Francine gave no sign of noticing any change in their demeanour, but Jessica, after studying them for some time, fell into a reverie and sat staring silently at the road ahead, a frown of concentration on her brow.

They left the waggon on the edge of a wood and walked up a short but steep slope to a clearing. Here Joss and Sebastian, having carried the things to a patch of grass, dropped their burdens, lit cigarettes and sat down to smoke abstractedly. Jessica made several attempts to rouse them, but after addressing them more than once and getting no reply, raised her eyebrows at Francine and without further comment helped her to unload the food. Having spread out the packages, she took the bottles of wine and walked down to cool them in the stream at the bottom of the slope. The two men stared absently, and then Sebastian rose, followed her a few paces and offered halfheartedly to do the task himself.

'Don't you bother,' she said. 'Just relax. Don't exhaust yourself; leave everything to the women.'

Even her tone failed to rouse him; he stood still for some minutes, looking in the direction in which she had gone, and then walked in slow circles round the clearing, lighting and throwing away cigarette after cigarette.

Joss sat leaning against a tree, his thoughts going round with a speed that bewildered him. Sebastian had told him to prepare words and he had spent a large part of the night in an effort to prepare them, but no words had come. He was to speak, and he could find nothing to say.

He had not needed to be told that he was in love. The vague, undefined restlessness that had filled him for the past week, the violent changes of mood from joy to depression, from moodiness to contentment, were symptoms he had never before experienced. His life had flowed smoothly, too smoothly, he had sometimes thought; as problems arose, he dealt with them with a speed and firmness which made his present indecision the more remarkable.

He wanted very much to marry; he had no desire to live by himself or to live for himself; somewhere deep within him was a conviction that he could make a success of marriage. A happy marriage, he believed, was the prize awarded to two people who had passed successfully one of life's most searching tests. He thought divorce deplorable; he had seen couples, friends of his, part for reasons which they considered sufficient but which he had felt to be totally inadequate. He believed, dimly and humbly, that he would make a good husband; he wanted to love and to cherish, to have and to hold, and with no nonsense, he

238

told himself, about putting asunder. He would put marriage first and himself next. It would work out.

If it came off, he concluded moodily. It would work out if it ever began.

A great desire for counsel rose in him. He was out of his depth and he was swimming aimlessly; he needed guidance and support. Sebastian's experience was wide, but it did not extend to proposals; it had not even reached, hitherto, beyond the frontiers of dalliance. A man, when he came to asking a girl to marry him, would find his own words and his own way, but there were things to be arranged first. One had to get the girl by herself in a suitable place and at a suitable time, and then the actual words of the proposal would without doubt come flowingly to the tongue. Even he, Joss, who fumbled and stumbled when there were pretty speeches to be made, even he would have the necessary address, he hoped, when the time for addressing arrived. But it would not arrive by itself; of this he was convinced. Men had to ... to manoeuvre.

Depression flooded him. Where, he asked himself, was the ecstasy? If he was on the verge of becoming engaged, where was the sense of elation, of longing, of hope, even of triumph? Was this lack of feeling, he asked himself miserably, the penalty for remaining so long a free man? He had not wanted to be free; he had wanted a wife and children and he had regretted the years that had passed without bringing them. But perhaps a man formed habits without knowing that he had formed them; perhaps this feeling of hesitation, of fear meant that he was unwilling, after all, to forego his freedom? The later, the harder, he had heard it said; now, with the hope of a lovely bride to urge him on, why did he not feel more? Why did he not, in fact, feel anything?

He decided that it was due to nothing more than nervousness. He could not feel, because he was thinking too much. And he was thinking to no purpose. If there had been anybody to give him one word of help or advice on the subject of proposals, a man or even a woman who could—

Jessica!

The name burst into his consciousness, scattering doubts, fears, hesitations. Of course Jessica would know! First because she was a woman, and women, they said, knew these things instinctively; but chiefly because she had been through one and probably many more experiences of this kind. She would know what led up to a proposal; she would be able to tell him how he could bridge the wide gulf between the unspoken and the spoken word. Of course—Jessica! She would help him.

He got up and went swiftly down the slope, his spirits becoming lighter at every step. He felt, now, no trace of hesitation; he walked with firmness and confidence.

He caught sight of Jessica as she reached the stream. He could see her as he neared the bottom of the slope; she was stooping to put the bottles into the cool water. He called, and she looked up and he ran the rest of the way and joined her. She looked at him with amusement in her eyes.

'Why all the haste?' she asked.

'I wanted . . . well, I wanted to ask you about something,' said Joss. 'I—'

He stopped, and despair crept over him once more. It had seemed a good idea to seek her advice, but now he was with her, he felt that she would despise him for his weakness and indecision.

'Well?' she prompted after a time.

She lifted a hand and brushed away, casually, a fly that hovered about his cheek. As he still stood unmoving, speechless, she let her eyes rove over him carelessly; she pulled out the flap of one of his pockets and picked a thread from his coat.

'Well?' she asked again.

Joss made the sternest effort of his life and managed to speak.

'It was . . . it was really nothing,' he said.

A strand of hair had fallen on to her forehead. He wanted, desperately, to lift it and put it back into place. Sebastian could have done it as kindly, as casually as she had just brushed away the fly. But he was unable to lift a finger. He would never, he realized with a sinking heart, he would never be able to lift a finger. Never. He was a man without courage, without—

'It must have been *something*,' said Jessica gently.

'No. No, it really wasn't,' said Joss.

'You mean you galloped down here because that fly was bothering you?'

'No.' He managed to smile. 'No. I did have something to ask you, but—It's no good, Jessica,' he said desperately. 'I'll never be ... articulate; never, never in all my life. It's no good. I came down to ask you how a man could get a girl alone long enough to ask her to m-marry him, and then I saw you and it all ... well, it all ... it ... all ...'

The words faltered and then died in his throat. She had taken a step towards him and her arms, her long, warm, lovely arms had slipped round his neck. Her cheek was against his and she was murmuring softly.

'Joss ... darling, darling Joss.'

He knew only that his heart was thumping in his ears. His arms closed round her automatically and tightened. He clung to her, and he knew that in the confusion of impressions, of sensations swirling round his mind, there was everything but indecision. He knew, now, what he wanted. He knew, now, why he had hesitated. Sebastian had diagnosed the complaint but had named the wrong cure. He had been unable to find words because he had been trying to imagine himself saying them—and it had been impossible to picture himself saying them to any other girl but the one he held now in his arms. She was in his arms and at this moment he could not have said how she had got there, but there she was, and never, so help him, would he let her go again. This had been the reason why he had felt nothing—because without Jessica in his arms, nothing had any meaning. Now he could speak. Now he could pour out what was in his heart. Now he could shout his love and his triumph. The words would flow like a torrent.

He took a deep breath.

'Oh ... Jessica,' he said.

They both waited for more, but nothing more came. And perhaps, thought Joss, it was all there, all in that one word.

She raised her head to look up at him.

'I never thought you'd get round to it,' she said gently. 'I thought I'd have to wait until we were on our way back to Jersey. I thought that if I could get you on deck and threaten to throw you overboard if you didn't tell me you loved me—Tell me now, please.'

'I love you with all my heart,' said Joss from his very depths. 'I've always—'

He stopped abruptly. Into the clear waters of his happiness there had fallen a pebble, and then a stone and then a rock. She was in his arms and—

'What's the matter?' she asked.

'It's ... it was only that I was thinking of ... of Sebastian.'

A slight frown appeared on her brow.

'Well, don't, darling,' she said. 'Why drag him in now? This is one time when you don't have to talk about Sebastian.'

'Yes. No. I mean, it was only ... I'd like him to be happy, and—'

'He'll be very happy, Joss darling. I told Francine not to hurry him. In some ways, he's not very bright; he's up to his ears in love with her.'

Joss stared down at her blankly.

'You mean he ... he doesn't know?' he brought out.

'Francine knows,' said Jessica. 'That's all that matters. Kiss me, Joss darling.'

She drew his reeling head down until his lips rested on hers.

Sebastian saw them as he reached the bottom of the slope. He had grown hungry, and then he had grown thirsty, and then he had grown impatient. Where was the wine? There had been time enough to cool it.

'I'll go and see what's happening,' he told Francine.

Having seen, he stood quite still.

So that was it, he understood at last. So it was Joss—and Jessica.

Joss and Jessica. Jessica and Joss. And up there in the clearing was Francine, alone. Francine—gentle, kind, lovely Francine was

244

up there, unsuspecting. It was not for her that Joss had been so unlike himself. He had smiled at Francine, walked with Francine, talked with her—and while he had walked and talked and smiled, it had been Jessica.

And Francine...

He could at least, thought Sebastian, turning and going blindly the way he had come, he could at least do something to prepare her, to warn her. He could go back and do something to shield her before those two walked up with their news written in flaming letters on their faces. He could stand between her and the first shock. Francine, gentle little Francine.

He was running. He cleared a boulder, missed the path and plunged into the thick wood. His speed increased; he was driven by a terrible feeling of urgency. Breathing noisily, he drove himself on.

But a wood is not, after all, a race track. He had almost reached the clearing when his foot caught in a sprawling root. He lurched, stumbled and went down; he saw a young sapling in his downward plunge, and jerked his head aside one second too late.

His next sensations were extremely pleasant. He was lying in Heaven, his head pillowed on a cloud. Angels were murmuring nearby, and every now and then one of the soft feathers from their wings dropped on to his face.

He opened his eyes. He was in Francine's arms; his head was pillowed on her breast; she was murmuring broken phrases into his ear. Every now and then a tear dropped from her cheek to his.

'Sebastian ... oh, Sebastian.'

And much more. He lay listening happily; how much softer, how much sweeter it all sounded in French. How lovely she was, how pure, how dear. Her face was above his; above her face, the pine trees; above the pine trees, the blue sky. A wave of humility engulfed him. Fool that he was, he had linked her in his mind with Joss, but Joss had proved that in matters of the heart he was not to be misled.

'Sebastian, are you hurt, my darling?'

'I'm ... I'm fine,' murmured Sebastian. He put up a hand and ran a finger down a strand of silken hair. 'Tante Francine, I love you very much.'

'Hush,' said Francine. 'Don't try to speak.'

'No. Will you marry me, Tante Francine?'

'Yes, yes,' soothed Francine. 'Hush.'

He sat up slowly and drew her into his arms.

'You are not hurt? Why did you run?' she asked.

'It was just that I ... that Joss—'

Francine put her lips gently on his and then drew back and looked at him with serious eyes.

'Don't go near,' she begged. 'Leave them for a little while and perhaps—You see, they love each other so much, but Joss is ... he is shy. Jessica will arrange everything.'

There was a long silence; she rested quietly in

246

his arms and only stirred when she saw a slow smile curving his lips.

'Why are you smiling?' she asked.

'Nothing. Just ... just women,' said Sebastian. 'You know something, Francine?'

'What, Sebastian?'

'I'm a big fool, that's what. But I'm willing to learn.'

CHAPTER FOURTEEN

On the day of the sale, there was a keen east wind blowing; Sebastian, having brought the yellow car round to the front of the chateau, went indoors to put a sweater under his jacket.

'Cold as that?' asked Joss.

'Yes. You'll need something. We ought to get going. Where's the Comtesse?'

They met her in the hall; she was still in the unchanging, unchanged black dress.

'I think you'll need a wrap of some sort,' said Joss.

'If you lived in this chateau, as I do, year after year, winter after winter,' said the Comtesse, 'you would not mind some healthy cold. But if you wish to nurse yourselves, I cannot prevent you.'

Nevertheless, when they had handed her into the car and Léon came hurrying out with a mangy-looking tippet, she did not refuse it.

247

Joss draped it round her shoulders and then got into the front beside Sebastian.

'I shall tell you the way,' said the Comtesse. 'When you get out of Cloisy, turn to the right.'

It was almost unnatural, thought Sebastian, to cross the bridge and pass the little lane without turning into it. Joss had the same feeling; he craned his neck for a sight of the pink house or its inmates, but saw nothing more than Maurice's small figure swinging from a tree.

'I suppose you look for your friend, Monsieur d'Arnaud,' observed the Comtesse with heavy sarcasm.

'Yes.' Sebastian's tone was casual. 'I'm going to marry his daughter.'

For the first time in their knowledge of her, the Comtesse sought for words and found none. Three kilometres, four, five passed in peaceful silence before she found her tongue.

'This is a joke!' she exclaimed at last.

'No joke,' said Sebastian, giving a happy little fanfare on the horn. 'Mademoiselle d'Arnaud is engaged to me.'

'And I'm going to marry Miss de Vrais,' said Joss.

There was another prolonged period of quiet.

'You have not wasted your time,' sniffed the Comtesse at last.

'No. It's been a most pleasant holiday, and we're very grateful to you,' said Sebastian.

'To me? For bringing you here? When you have been married for ten years, see if you are still grateful to me. I do not understand how old d'Arnaud can be at ease over this. The father of the other girl has shown that he has no control over her, but old d'Arnaud to permit his daughter to marry a stranger, that I cannot understand. In England and in America, young men and women, after one glance, throw themselves one on to the other's neck, but here in France I thought that there would be still some dignity, some patience, some formalities. Perhaps he is failing, old d'Arnaud, to allow this.'

'Mademoiselle d'Arnaud,' said Joss, 'will be very well cared for, and very happy.'

'I am sure that you think so, as her fiancé is your friend. But allow me to say that in two weeks one cannot build a marriage.'

'No. One can only lay the foundations,' said Sebastian. 'And that's all we've done, and as you brought us here, the credit must go to you.'

'Thank you. I do not wish for credit,' said the Comtesse. 'If you wish for my congratulations, of course I must give them, but do not ask for my approval.'

Nobody did; they drove on in silence until they came to the outskirts of La Rochelle, and then the Comtesse leaned forward to direct Sebastian.

'There, that is the gate.'

The house was very large, and crowded to

capacity by buyers from all parts of the country. The Comtesse fought her way through the throng in the hall and made her way by slow degrees up the stairs. Joss watched her with admiration.

'Hatpin, I shouldn't wonder,' he murmured. 'She—' He turned. 'Oh, good morning, Madame Jules.'

Madame Jules smiled at them.

'It is cold.' She gave a shudder. 'So cold, and such a crowd. We shall have to wait a little; everybody is trying to get in at once. And while we wait, I shall congratulate you both.'

'When did you hear about it?' asked Joss.

'Early this morning, when I was dressing. Francine came to see me. I have promised, of course, to take care of her father as tenderly as she has done. You are both very fortunate men. And now I must go and get Hubert. He is in my car; I did not allow him to get out until his aunt was out of the way.'

'What did you tell him?' asked Joss.

'I told him that I am anxious to keep this screen in our family, and will pay anything to do so. It is going to be interesting, I think. It will also be expensive—for me or for the Comtesse. We shall see.'

When it came to the turn of the screen to be auctioned, the Comtesse, in her corner of the large room, showed no special interest in the proceedings. Only when the bidding became high and all but formidable competition had

250

dropped away did she make a sign to the auctioneer.

'Four hundred thousand francs,' he intoned. 'I am offered four hundred thousand francs.'

There was a pause. The auctioneer was looking round, but there seemed to be no advance in the bidding.

'Four hundred thousand ... five.'

The Comtesse glanced casually over her shoulder in the direction of the bidder. She had looked once more at the auctioneer and raised a hand before the significance of what she had seen seemed to strike her. Her head turned slowly once more and she stared unbelievingly.

Hubert was leaning negligently against a seventeenth-century tallboy. He straightened to bow coldly to his aunt, looked over her shoulder to raise the bidding and then sank back against the tallboy.

There was a tense silence; the Comtesse seemed mesmerized. A change in the auctioneer's voice roused her and she swung round in time to raise the bidding once more. Then she was pushing her way through the crowd, thrusting with shoulder and elbow; those in her way, sensing drama, suffered her buffeting in silence. She came to a halt beside Hubert, and he raised a careless hand.

'Nine hundred thousand francs,' chanted the auctioneer. 'I am offered nine hundred thousand francs for—'

'Are you mad?' hissed the Comtesse to

251

Hubert. 'Shall I have to call the police? You are insane, and I shall end this farce and—' She swung round desperately and raised a hand.

'One million francs,' sang the auctioneer. 'I am offered one million francs for the screen. I am—'

'This will stop,' ground out the Comtesse, facing Hubert. 'You are penniless. You—'

'Certainly I am penniless. But I do not bid for myself,' he told her coolly. 'I am bidding for someone who has a very special reason for buying this screen.'

The Comtesse did not need to ask who it was. She had seen, across the room, the small, exquisite figure of Madame Jules. There was no need to look twice to see the confidence of her bearing or the look of mockery in her eye.

The Comtesse took a deep breath. Her thoughts raced; fury and fear warred in her mind—and fear won. This was not the Hubert she knew. This was not the cringing young man she had grown to despise. Always good-looking, he had in the past few minutes taken on a dignity and an assurance which reminded her not unpleasantly of the late Comte. He was not acting; he was facing her with emotions which she recognized as genuine: dislike, defiance and ... yes, contempt. The worm had not only turned; it was standing up and asserting its rights. Backed by Madame Jules, Hubert, it was clear, was calm and unafraid. He was bidding for the screen and—

'You would do this to me, your aunt?' she asked hoarsely.

'Certainly.' Hubert raised two fingers at the auctioneer. 'Certainly. This is what I have always wanted to do—to buy and sell—but you would not let me. I advise you to make your bid quickly; everybody is waiting.'

The Comtesse took a crumpled handkerchief from her handbag and wiped her glistening forehead. Her eyes went to the auctioneer and she gave a tremulous nod. Then she turned back to Hubert and spoke firmly.

'If you will stop bidding,' she said, 'you may make your own terms.'

'To live at the chateau and refurnish part of it.' Hubert gave the auctioneer another casual nod. 'To bid for you and earn a reasonable commission. To live according to my station.'

'But—'

'The auctioneer is waiting.'

The Comtesse turned and nodded slowly. A few moments later, the screen was hers.

She stood beside Hubert and they looked at one another in silence for a time, and some dim feeling of future benefits crept into her mind. With the knowledge of strong support, he had shown firmness and resolution. He was weak, but he could be propped up. He was useless without backing, but given it, he could look and behave almost like a man. A hazy realization of his possible usefulness stirred and took root; she was old; Léon was old; life was not gay there in the vast and cheerless chateau, and although she did not want Hubert's company, perhaps it would be better than none.

'You have promised,' said Hubert, 'that I shall come back to live at the chateau. Are you going to keep your word?'

For a moment, the Comtesse hesitated. He had found a rich patron, and for the sake of coming back to live at the chateau, he had destroyed his credit and in doing so had robbed an old enemy of a chance to score.

'Do I ever,' she demanded, 'go back on my word?'

'Of course. But this time,' said Hubert, 'I do not think that you will. There are many things that I can arrange for you.'

She did not reply. She straightened her hat, sent a last fierce glare across to the small figure on the other side of the room, and prepared to push her way out.

'I will wait for you downstairs,' she told Hubert. 'Kindly do all that is necessary here.'

'Send the two Englishmen back with Madame Jules,' said Hubert in a new tone of command. 'I will drive you home. And in future, I think that we shall use the green car. It is more suitable. It is a good thing that I bought it for us.'

*   *   *

But it was the yellow car in which he offered to drive Joss and Sebastian to St Malo.

'We won't all fit in,' pointed out Sebastian.

'You are all going together?' enquired Hubert.

'Yes. At least, we're all going to St Malo together. Five of us. Joss and Jessica are going to get the boat to Jersey, and are taking Maurice with them. But before they go, they're going to see Francine and myself off at the airport; we're flying to London.'

'Francine is going with you?'

'She's going on a visit to my parents.'

'Then I shall take you all. I shall put a luggage rack on top of the car.'

'That's very decent of you,' said Sebastian.

'It will not be too expensive,' went on Hubert. 'You will have the first use of it, so perhaps you will pay something. And for the petrol, of course, both ways, because I shall have to come back here after taking you.'

'Well ... thanks,' said Sebastian. 'But perhaps a taxi would—'

'No. You must permit me,' said Hubert, 'because I feel an especial interest in you all. Once Jessica loved me, but we must forget that. It is something that could not be helped. I am not going to say that Frenchmen are irresistible; I will say only that English girls find them so. She was not to blame. Simply, she was infatuated. And Francine will be very happy. For myself, I could not marry her because how

255

should we have lived on nothing? I am not saying that she loved me, but—'

'Infatuated, simply?' asked Sebastian.

'Yes. Do not say this to her.'

'Won't breathe a word,' promised Sebastian.

They repeated the conversation to Jessica when Hubert was out of the way.

'His aunt,' she commented, 'will find that she's swallowed a viper.'

'You don't swallow them; you nurse them,' said Sebastian. 'Which brings me to the subject of the vipers who try to do the Customs people down. What's going to be done about getting those jewels back to where they came from?'

'I brought them; I'll take them back,' said Jessica. 'I'm not frightened.'

'But I am,' said Joss. 'I love you very much, but I'm not prepared to go through the Customs with you knowing that you're carrying contraband—not that kind of contraband, anyhow. When you came, it was more or less plain sailing; you were telling the truth and those men are trained to read signs. They can tell.'

'I'm going to be married, and I can tell them so.'

'You won't convince them,' said Sebastian, 'that you came over to France for a fortnight to pick up a wedding dress. The whole thing will give off an odour of cod. So I've got a few suggestions for the best way of getting the stuff

256

through.'

'Let's have them,' said Joss.

'A Thermos flask isn't a bad way,' said Sebastian. 'You take out the inside and pop in the jewels and—'

'No,' said Jessica.

'Well, there's another way. My old man, who's normally law-abiding,' said Sebastian, 'got stuck once with an expensive watch from Geneva and—'

'You mean he bought himself a watch in Geneva?' corrected Jessica.

'That's what I said. He couldn't wear it, because he was wearing two already, one on each hand, and he got the extra one through by rolling it inside a pair of socks. Then there was another fellow who—'

'You needn't go on,' said Joss. 'I'm going to take the jewels from Jessica and I'm going to put them back, personally, in her father's safe. How I do it is my own affair. I have a plan, but I have no intention of telling anybody about it.'

'Have it your own way,' said Sebastian. 'But when you're paying the fine, don't say I wasn't prepared to help you. One more thing. When Francine comes back to Cloisy, I'm coming with her. We'd like to come back by way of Jersey; if Jessica will put Francine up, I'll have my usual bed at the cottage. All right?'

It was all right. Satisfied, Sebastian went to tell Francine of the arrangements, and Jessica looked at Joss.

'Can you believe,' she said slowly, 'that we'll soon be back in Jersey? Isn't it wonderful?'

'It would be,' said Joss, 'except for that nice, friendly talk I've got to have with your father. If he calls me a fortune-hunter, I'll—'

'You'll what?'

'I'll think of something.'

'Joss.' Her voice was sober. 'I was thinking, in the night, of you and me, and how we met, and I got frightened thinking what a hit-and-miss affair it all was. We left Jersey on the same day, on the same boat, but if I hadn't quarrelled with Hubert, if the Comtesse hadn't been there, if ... if ... if ...'

'Yes. It's a chancy business,' agreed Joss. 'But we'd probably have met in Jersey one day. All the same, it seems a bit haphazard; for one couple who meet, there must be millions who just miss it. The thing ought to be better organized. The only thing ...' He had drawn her into his arms and his voice was lost in her hair. 'Darling, what makes you smell so sweet?'

'Francine's powder,' said Jessica.

CHAPTER FIFTEEN

The yellow car arrived in good time, but Francine and Jessica and Maurice were ready, and their luggage assembled in the hall. Francine was in a loose coat and a beret; it was

258

the first time Sebastian had seen her in anything but light summer dresses, and he kissed her soberly, fighting down a longing to pick her up and carry her out of sight and tell her what he thought of this new and even lovelier Francine.

'You look very nice in a beret,' was all he said.

'So does Joss.' Jessica held out the black beret she was holding. 'Put it on, Joss.'

Sebastian stared at him in amazement.

'You're going to wear a beret?' he asked.

'Why not?' demanded Jessica. 'He wanted one, and we bought one and he looks jolly nice in it. Put it on, darling.'

Somewhat sheepishly, Joss placed his new headgear at what he hoped was a becoming angle on his head. Jessica and Francine adjusted it and Hubert gave it a finishing touch or two.

'I feel terrible,' said Joss.

'You look terrible,' said Sebastian. 'Where's Maurice disappeared to?'

'He's saying good-bye to my father. I'll bring him out with me,' said Francine.

The others walked out to the car; Maurice ran to join them and soon Francine came out of Monsieur d'Arnaud's room and walked to the gate. There was no sign of her father; he had made his formal farewells on the previous night and he preferred now to say good-bye to his daughter in the privacy of his little room.

Sebastian took Francine's hand in his.

'All right?' he asked.

She nodded and smiled.

'Then let's go. You and Jessica on the big seats at the back, with Joss and Maurice on the two little seats. Me in front, in comfort, with Hubert.'

They got in, and then there was the small matter of a parting present for Céline. This having been seen to satisfactorily by Joss and Sebastian, they left her bobbing with pleasure at the gate, and then they were backing down the little lane and turning in the direction of the coast.

'Did you say good-bye nicely to the Comtesse?' Jessica asked Joss.

A crimson flush overspread his cheeks.

'She kissed us,' he said. 'On both cheeks.'

There was no comment; everybody sat silent, picturing the Comtesse's farewell.

It was very windy at the airport; Sebastian, for the first time, saw the advantages of a beret and said so to Joss.

'I'll let you borrow mine—but not today,' said Joss.

Something in his tone made Sebastian look at him curiously.

'Why not today, particularly?' he asked.

'Today I just happen to need it, that's all,' said Joss.

Sebastian looked at the beret. There was nothing of especial note about it, except the fact that it looked somewhat too big for its wearer; the top was flat and smooth, but round the edges was a suggestion of bulginess, even of bulkiness. Sebastian, staring at the bulges, gave a sudden exclamation and put out a hand to feel them, and Joss took a quick step backward.

'Hands off,' he said.

Sebastian began to laugh, and Joss laughed with him. The sound of their laughter, deep and prolonged, reached Jessica and she left Francine and Maurice with Hubert and came across to find out the cause of the amusement.

'It's Joss.' Sebastian gave another roar of laughter. 'The beret.'

Jessica slipped her arm into Joss's.

'He said he'd think of a way of fixing the contraband, and he thought of a way and I'm very proud of him,' she said. 'I think it's the best way anybody could have done it.'

'It was Joss's idea, was it?' asked Sebastian.

'My idea entirely,' said Joss. 'There's your flight number. See you both in Jersey.'

Sebastian took Francine's arm and followed the air hostess to the waiting plane. A sense of unreality filled him. Two weeks ... it was two weeks since he had left England, and he was returning with Francine. He was no longer a man without a goal, without a purpose; he was engaged and he would shortly be married. He wondered what his parents were thinking; his letters from Lysaine could not have been too coherent.

They landed on schedule. Sebastian walked beside Francine to the airport buildings and felt excitement rising in him. His eyes went to the people waiting to meet the passengers, and after a brief search he found the two figures he was looking for and raised a hand in greeting.

'There, darling, look. Mother and the old man.'

He turned to exhibit his prize, but Francine had been shepherded to the place reserved for aliens and was for the moment lost to him. She joined him in the Customs shed and he took her hand.

'Mother and the old man are out there,' he told her.

A faint colour came into her cheeks, and her eyes went to his for reassurance.

'They'll love you,' he said. 'As soon as we get out of here—'

A hatred of delays, of formalities, swept over him. He was on English soil, but before he could walk freely upon it, he must await the word of the authorities. He choked down his impatience and bent to assist Francine as the Customs official paused before them.

'Got your keys, darling?'

'Yes. But this case is not locked,' said Francine, in her careful, pretty English.

She opened the case and raised calm blue eyes to the Customs officer. Sebastian, looking at the man's face, saw the subtle change in it and glanced down at the case. He felt his mouth go dry.

To right and left, the sudden hush, the heads turning, those nearby closing in to get a better view. Yard upon yard of foaming white tulle, rising, billowing. In the centre, gently laid upon the topmost fold, a small circlet of orange blossom.

The blood drummed in Sebastian's ears. He stood fighting to control his expression, his bearing; the slightest tensing could bring disaster. He was numb with terror and helplessness, sweating with foreboding.

The Customs official was looking at Francine out of keen, clear, intelligent grey eyes. He looked entirely unmoved. His voice was brisk. His hand went out and fingered one of the folds.

'You're French?' he asked Francine.

She nodded.

'Going to get married?'

'Yes, monsieur. To this gentleman.'

The gentleman, by clinging desperately to the side of the counter, prevented himself from giving a wild cry and rushing out of the building.

'Wedding dress?' enquired the official.

'Yes, monsieur. But it is not French material. The material is English; it was not made in France. It is English and it was given to me as a present.'

The man nodded. The case was closed and

chalked. If Sebastian's luggage was examined, he did not know it; he was incapable of thought. He found himself walking beside Francine; she was saying something.

'It was Joss's idea,' she told him.

Sebastian remembered Jessica's words; she, too, had given Joss the credit. He recalled the note of pride in her voice, and marvelled at his own simplicity. It was not the first time he had been on the receiving end of one of Joss's jokes; it would not be the last. He would deal with Joss when he got to Jersey.

He looked down at Francine.

'Why didn't you give the things to me to look after?' he asked.

'Joss said that if you knew I had them, you would be unable to prevent yourself from looking anxious on my account. He said that you would worry a great deal. I was not anxious,' she said calmly, 'because I spoke only the truth. I said nothing that was not true. Did I, Sebastian?'

He took her hand in his.

'Nothing, darling,' he said.

Two people came forward eagerly to meet them, and Sebastian drew Francine forward.

'Here she is,' he told them simply.

We hope you have enjoyed this Large Print book. Other Chivers Press or Thorndike Press Large Print books are available at your library or directly from the publishers. For more information about current and forthcoming titles, please call or write, without obligation, to:

Chivers Press Limited
Windsor Bridge Road
Bath BA2 3AX
England
Tel. (0225) 335336

OR

Thorndike Press
P.O. Box 159
Thorndike, ME 04986
USA
Tel. (800) 223-6121
(207) 948-2962
(in Maine and Canada, call collect)

All our Large Print titles are designed for easy reading, and all our books are made to last.